WHEN
GOD
WAS A
BOY

"And Yeshua increased in wisdom and stature..."

*LUKE 2:52

WHEN GOD WAS A BOY

C.T. GILES

ISBN: 979-8-9851493-0-2 (Hardcover)
ISBN: 979-8-9851493-1-9 (Ebook)
ISBN: 979-8-9851493-2-6 (Audiobook)

Library of Congress Control Number: 2022901887

This book is a work of fiction. Any references to historical events, real people, or real places are used fictitiously. Other names, characters, places and events are products of the author's imagination, and any resemblance to actual events, places or persons, living or dead, is entirely coincidental.

Front cover images © Shutterstock
Book design by *the*BookDesigners
Edited by Barbara Kois
Historical Advisor, Mark S. Kinzer

Printed in the United States of America.

First printing edition 2022

SOULWRIGHTS
Soulwrights Press
PO Box 1418
Lynchburg, VA 24505

www.soulwrights.org

In memory of James Murray Terris, Jr., my Grampy,
who taught me so much about words, music and chess.

Epigraph

CONSIDER THE CALLING of Joseph. Every vocation is unique – in the sense that the Good Shepherd calls each of his sheep by its own proper name – but there was something supremely unique in the vocation of Joseph, who was called to be the foster father of God's Son and the protector of that divine Son's virgin mother. Joseph's vocation was not only difficult; it was impossible! In a sense, Joseph had to figure it out as he went along, simply following God's call, as best he could, wherever it led. He was obliged to leave the heavy lifting to God.

With so distinctive and demanding a vocation, Joseph might be excused, if, on occasion – the flight into Egypt, for instance – he felt anxious and insecure. The evidence, however, indicates that this was not the case. Joseph was not a person given to anxiety. He appeared, rather, as a man of extraordinary serenity. We find Joseph in five scenes in the gospel of Matthew, and every single time he is sound asleep (Matthew 1:20-24; 2:12, 13, 19, 22). Whatever troubles Joseph endured, they did not include insomnia.

Perhaps we see Joseph's mark on Jesus – particularly the example of his serenity and simple trust in God – when we contemplate a later New Testament scene:

Now when they had left the multitude, they took Jesus along in the boat as he was. And other little boats were also with him. And a great windstorm arose, and the waves beat into the boat, so that it was already filling. But he was in the stern, asleep on a pillow. (Mark 4:36-38)

Patrick Henry Reardon
THE JESUS WE MISSED

Contents

Endorsements

C.T. Giles is a gifted storyteller and wordsmith. In this engaging midrashic narrative of the young Yeshua's relationship to Yosef and Miriam, Giles remains faithful to the biblical text while spinning a tale set in its intriguing gaps. Giles portrays a youthful Messiah whose Jewishness, displayed in the rich concrete details of his daily life, is not an incidental accident of birth but an essential feature of his identity and vocation. This Yeshua is believably human *and* believably divine. But the real hero of the story is Yosef, who must contend with a parental task greater than any father had ever faced before. Read, learn, be inspired, enjoy.

—MARK S. KINZER, Ph.D.
Rabbi Emeritus of Congregation Zera Avraham, Author of *Jerusalem Crucified, Jerusalem Risen:*
The Resurrected Messiah, the Jewish People, and the Land of Promise

The church, the synagogue, and the world need a Jewish Jesus, and C.T. Giles has given us a picture of this Jesus as a boy of thirteen. Laying tefillin, reciting berachot, and discoursing with the rabbis on matters of Torah, Yeshua of Nazareth is portrayed here as he truly lived: as a devout first-century Jew who never abandoned his zeal for the Torah. Through the eyes of his father Yosef, we sense the young Messiah's wisdom and alacrity along with the inner turmoil that came from being born under the heavy burden of prophecy. Giles's flowing prose inspires us to imagine how Yeshua's family would have navigated their kingly ancestry, their hope of national restoration, and their subjection to the Romans, all critical contexts for understanding the teachings of Yeshua in the Gospels. The deceptively simple narrative cloaks a deep exploration into the trials of the Jewish people in first-century rural Galilee and suggests how these trials might have shaped the worldview of our Messiah. Inspiring and evocative, *When God Was a Boy* is a must-read for anyone who wants to see their vision of the Jewish Jesus sharpened and clarified.

—BOAZ MICHAEL
Founder and President of First Fruits of Zion, Author of *Tent of David*

How does one attempt to write a fictional account of the shrouded, early life of Jesus? In accepting an incredibly daunting challenge, Giles has brought to life my imagination. The read was a riveting story and joyful adventure. But this exercise in imagination was not simply entertainment, it was also instructive and provoked reflection in me that helped me to grow in my relationship with the non-fictional Jesus.

—MARTY SOLOMON
Creator and Executive Producer of the BEMA Podcast

This fresh telling of the life and story of Joseph is a wonderful gift from C.T. Giles. This book literally makes the reader feel as if they are right there with Jesus and his father Joseph. It humanizes the father/son relationship in such a beautiful way. Excited for this book to make its way into people's hands and hearts!

—MARK HARRIS
Executive Pastor of Worship at Gateway Church, founding member of 4Him

We read aloud *When God Was a Boy* as a family. When I say it has been a beautiful guide and companion to our family, imagining what it might have been like in 1st century Nazareth, watching Jesus come of age, I'm only scratching the surface. We have laughed and cried through this book, brought into quiet and worshipful spaces in every chapter, and only wanted to read more at every turn. This was an instant classic in our home that we will return to annually, no doubt about it!

—RAYNNA MYERS
mom of six, blogger at www.raynnamyers.com, Author of *Beloved Prayers*

Have you ever taken a left hook to the liver? It is the kind of shot that sticks with you, having the uncanny ability to shock you and then leave you paralyzed. From an emotional perspective, that was my experience with this book. I found myself consistently staying up way too late (at the dismay of my work the next day) just reading and re-reading chapters. I'm not sure I knew how little I had imagined beforehand – what it meant for the Messiah to come of age. Reading this book has brought the Bible, previously lost on my context, to new life by the imagination of the author. I've laughed, yelled, and cried reading this book.

I realized how brave and honorable my step-father was the day I got married. The realization came when I empathized that the day he said "I do" all those years ago, he not only became a husband for the first time, but he immediately became a father as well. I had a similar experience with Yosef in this story. For the first time, I sat in the space of empathy of what it must have been like to be the adoptive father of the Messiah. This book is an absolute must read. C.T. Giles is a radically gifted storyteller. His work brought me into a deeper appreciation of YHWH and His ordination within Yeshua's family. *When God Was a Boy* is a masterpiece that will lead you to deeper worship of the Father.

—MARSHALL SHANK
Director of Outreach, Proven Men Ministries

One chapter left me choking back tears; another left me breathless and paralyzed. Every chapter bore a gift, drawing me deeper into the heart of Yeshua and fanning the flames of my love for and devotion to him. C.T. Giles brilliantly sets each scene to re-present life in first century Nazareth, a community of Jews living under Roman occupation. Center stage, he captures the shrewd brilliance of Yeshua and his unceasing compassion, the loving intent of Father God behind the Law, and the necessity of properly translating Scripture against the metanarrative of the Sacred Text. Pictures of raw humanity encircle the central drama, bringing to life real people in a real place at a real time in history with real relationships: husbands and wives, parents and children, neighbors and friends, even dangerous enemies. While *When God Was a Boy* is an imaginative work of fiction it authentically captures "how it might have unfolded," tracing Gospel-documented events backwards... like threads looking for their knotted anchor. Giles's literary offering also challenges readers who follow Yeshua (if readers will allow it) to explore what it might look like to faithfully walk out Yeshua's radical call to live as he lived, to do as he does. If Giles decides to write a sequel, rest assured, it will be on my "must read next!" list.

—MONICA WARREN
speaker, Ironman triathlete, blogger @ www.hijackedjesus.com,
Author of *A Search for the Real Jesus*

I have so often wondered what the life of Jesus was like when He was a boy. Scripture jumps from his boyhood teaching in the Temple to his adult Baptism by his cousin and has left me oftentimes wondering about the answer to that question... What happened in all of those in-between years? Those in-between years that we all know are critical to the development of our character and understanding of this world. I don't think those years were any exception to Jesus and I take great comfort in that. In *When God Was a Boy*, author C.T. Giles paints us a suggested picture of those years that are incredibly real, raw, harrowing, and also incredibly beautiful. This is not just a make-believe story about what Jesus may have been like as a young man, but it is a well-researched historical fiction account that gave me a newfound connection to Jesus. Giles gives the reader a front row seat witnessing the life of young Jesus from the perspective of Joseph, someone we don't hear too much from in Scripture. For example, watching Jesus love his parents well, while also struggling with the complexities of those relationships gave me a much-needed appreciation for his humanity as well as our similarities when it comes to relationships with loved ones. Also, to read about Jesus being targeted by those in power who wanted to hurt him inspired me to continue spending my life advocating for vulnerable people who are exploited by the powerful. The examples could go on and on... and that is why *When God Was a Boy* is such an important read for those who find themselves struggling or just curious to understand and reconcile Jesus as young man and Jesus as God.

Even though *When God Was a Boy* is historical fiction, I couldn't help but walk with a sense of hope that perhaps it's more historical than fiction. Bravo to C.T. Giles for giving us the opportunity to finally experience Jesus as a young man who reminds us of ourselves and our great God in both beautiful and mysterious ways.

—BOZ TCHIVIDJIAN
advocate and attorney for sexual abuse victims,
founder of GRACE: Godly Response to Abuse in the Christian Environment

As a father and grandfather, I found myself reflecting and relating to Joseph's emotions, thoughts and actions regarding raising a child. Yet I could not fully grasp the complete range this father was experiencing. How could I as he was fulfilling an unprecedented role of raising the messiah! I found myself switching from compatibility to intrigued foreign spectator! This story ended too soon.

—SAL FERLISE
CEO Sports Outreach Institute

C.T. Giles has masterfully woven together a tale of relationships, history, and adventure. *When God Was a Boy* prompted in me a meaningful questioning of everything I know of not only the human personality of the Lord, but those closest to him when he was young. I felt transported to a time in the life of Yeshua that I have often wondered about. In this telling, the author fills a gap in documented history with a wonderful slice of uplifting imagination.

—BENJI SHEPHERD
On Air Personality and Promotions Director, The JOY FM Georgia

We've all read the Bible stories of Jesus. Maybe we've even seen stories about how Mary treasured the memories of the baby Jesus in her heart. But have you ever pondered how Joseph felt about his son? C.T. Giles takes on the incredible challenge of showing us the teenager Jesus through the eyes of his earthly father, Joseph. The story comes off as familiar but riveting. You think you know what's next, but then Giles takes things on a left turn. He deftly blends the dramatic story of life in first-century occupied Israel with a Jesus who has an entirely different understanding of what it means to be the Messiah than his closest family. *When God Was a Boy* will awaken you to see Jesus with brand new eyes and to experience his story in a whole new way.

—JERRY WOODS
Morning Show Host, WGTS 91.9, Washington, D.C.

No one reads the Bible uninterpreted. In fact, the Bible seems to encourage all to read with their lens on and with creative imagination. C.T. Giles masterfully paints vivid imaginative snapshot stories of *When God Was a Boy* with such lively studious details as if we are reading portions of the Bible we somehow missed. The Gospels have scanty stories of Yeshua when he was young. Giles helps us to imagine the very Yeshua that we've come to love and follow. Yeshua was religious and irreligious at the same time, which is to say, He was traditional and revolutionary simultaneously. His life of being and doing, ultimately becoming, flowed naturally out of His oneness with God the Father, without ever demeaning relationship with His earthly father, Yosef. Yeshua was a perfect Son to God the Father and a perfect son to Yosef and Miriam. Yeshua's authentic humanity, sometimes wild and sometimes mundane and sometimes extraordinary, is what draws us to Him. I heartily recommend this book for those who are already on the journey of discovering Yeshua and our true selves as well as for those who need encouragement to do so.

—CHONG KIM
Plural Leadership Director at Frontier Ventures

The Biblical story claims Yeshua was fully human – but rarely do we contemplate what that would have been *really* like, especially when he was young. In *When God Was a Boy* Giles masterfully reveals the unvarnished world of 1st century Natzeret in Roman occupied Israel. He laser beams in on Yeshua's 13th year, with great insight and empathy from the perspective of his earthly father, Yosef. His fictional but wonderfully detailed, historically grounded narrative boldly tackles the daily, real-life confusion of parenting a young Messiah, especially how to prepare him to be Israel's deliverer. Giles also gives us a glimpse into adolescent Yeshua's developing understanding of who he is – and his call to die, out of love, for his people. I laughed... I raged... I wept... C.T. Giles's attempt to bring a forgotten piece of redemption history to life will remind you, maybe more deeply than ever, of why you fell in love with Jesus of Nazareth in the first place. By the last line, your heart will long for more.

—J. KEVIN BUTCHER
pastor, Author of *Choose & Choose Again* and *Free*

1

A Boy in His Father's Workshop

THE MAN WAS a forgettable kind of handsome possessed of an uncanny measure of virtue. He did not stand out in a crowd even though his destiny would outstrip everyone in his generation. His face was unremarkable – wavy-brown hair and golden-brown eyes, a broad forehead, a soft, angular nose, although his beard was majestic, full and billowing all the way down to his chest. And the laugh-lines in his face were set deep into his cheeks and eyes, like trenches laid out long in the hard-fought war against sorrows. Centuries would pass before his importance to humanity would become known to the world. Yet this was a man born between the turning of the ages, brought into being to become the pilot at the helm of history.

His peers respected him more than his station in life warranted. His friends deferred to him in conversation. The other Torah teachers heeded his reflections in the synagogue. People found an enveloping comfort in his company. More often than not, he was on the listening end of things. Simply put, people were delighted to be drawn to him, usually without knowing why.

He was descended from a great line of kings – and he carried himself like he knew it. The nobility on his brow was humble although heavy with forgotten glories. One might think that his coronation ceremony would happen the next day, if they did not also know the manner of poverty that colored his life.

No matter what, whether with friend or stranger, he had a numinous presence that hovered over him, like the pillar of fire that went before the Hebrews in the Wilderness so many ages ago. His character was expansive; his love was wide; his understanding was ever-deepening. Indeed, he was possessed of many inestimable qualities, any one of which would set a soul apart for greatness, and he carried them all together in concert without pride.

Nevertheless, there was a single fact that eclipsed anything else that one could know about him. One truth would shape his entire reality, demand his undying fealty, determine his unalterable trajectory. Ultimately, only one thing really mattered.

Yosef was the surrogate father of the messiah – and no one could know their secrets.

Their home was situated near the bottom of the town's embankments. Uphill from their modest hovel, Yosef scampered down the uneven steps of stone slabs like a soldier charging down into a valley, hurtling through the steep descents with deft agility. He gripped the new paring chisel in hand as if it were his unsheathed weapon in battle. Yosef was not angry, neither was he in a terrible hurry. He simply liked to run, especially when it meant running to synagogue or running home. The rocky, precipitous terrain of Natzeret made the exercise difficult to perform. However, to chase after those places as a habit, he found that even when he was prohibited from running in a given moment, as when carrying a child or some other precious burden, his heart still quickened as he headed in the right direction. He had trained his body to anticipate the haunts to which he should return.

Sometimes his wife Miriam tutted at him for the dirt that he kicked up into his tallit, the simple four-cornered cloak that draped over most of his torso. She had woven the outer garment herself in secret over the course of an entire year. It was modest enough compared to some of the other Pharisees, only covering him down below his hips (she had seen some that dragged the ground). Nonetheless it was exquisite in its attention to detail. Every thread and stitch were accounted for, with fastidious attention to the tassels and knots of the tzitzit at the fringes of the tallit. Miriam relished the thought that her love continued to cover Yosef once he left the house for the day, not to mention the presence of HaShem Himself, the God of Yisrael. So, it was understandable that she made a fuss over his regular staining.

Every time, Yosef looked a little embarrassed, like a child caught in his mischief. But he was quick on his feet. He simply smiled and reassured Miriam that he couldn't help being in a hurry to see her. She would tsk at the overture, but she would lean in for his kiss, too.

The children had seen the routine many times. Everyone knew the choreography. Abba would get in trouble; Ima would succumb to his charms. No one ever tired of the dance, least of all the kisser, or the kissed.

The carpenter had just returned from the blacksmith. Yeshua, his son, had become a fine woodworker, skilled and diligent beyond his years. He was also becoming stronger every day. Sometimes his strength got away from him. The most recent broken tool was yet another unexpected expense. Such had been the days of late.

These were trying times for Yosef. The endless cycle of work to do and mouths to feed. His family always had enough in the end, that much was true. But they ever so rarely had plenty. Too often, it seemed, it was a convoluted exercise to be content. Still, he carried on, as though he were a lord living in squalor.

His lot in life as a craftsman was that of so many others working in the trades, in that he was constructing much more valuable things for his clients than he would ever possess for his own family. Their house was no exception, downsized for the poor, divided into a meager two bedrooms and one common area for living and dining. Inside it was just barely tall enough for the average adult to stand up. The edifice was all wood and stone, unhewn and dry-stacked, yet impervious to the elements. Oftentimes the flat rooftop was the coolest place in the house.

Their hovel was one of many scores within the township of Natzeret. The grandiosity of its name by far outshone the meagerness of its municipality. With its rugged landscape and strenuous climbs, it was a nicer place to visit than it was to inhabit. Most of its thousand some residents were descendants of King David, and they fancied themselves as harbingers and progenitors of the coming messiah. It pained Yosef to know the truth and to be prohibited from announcing its nearness.

The Nazarenes were devout, sturdy, industrious people. Everyone farmed, although several of the clans were made up of tradesmen as well. With stone homes built atop the porous rock of their land, virtually all of the houses contained riches and provisions beneath the surface, having cisterns, vaults and silos to contain their water, grains, wine and oils. The difficulty of the above-ground craggy living was offset by the advantages that the below-ground rock formations afforded. The town, like its people, contained substance hidden from plain view.

Yosef collected himself for just a moment before he entered the workshop. He had been deliberating over something for a few months and had only recently decided to address his son about the matter of his eventual kingship. As far as Yosef was concerned, the timbers of Yeshua's character were more than seasoned for the work of his preparation. Yeshua was the messiah, after all; Israel's future could not wait but so long.

When he was most honest with himself, Yosef had to admit that he did not know what formal preparations for the messiah looked like, not entirely. But he did have some clear notions of the sorts of training that his son should be given to: military command, rhetoric, trade, economics, governance of domestic affairs. By Yosef's estimation, they were grossly behind schedule in what he supposed was the curriculum for a king-to-be.

Had his son even been in a fistfight? How in Heaven's Glory was he supposed to muster an army to lead against the Romans with not so much as a black eye or a bloody nose to his name? Surely, Rome would not be preached into submission.

Enough time had gone by. Yosef resolved within himself once again to confront Yeshua with the grave seriousness of the matter so that they might begin to build a plan. After all, his people had been waiting for their deliverer far too long as it was. Inasmuch as it was up to him to determine, Yosef would not have the messiah pass through his own household without direction. The fate of his nation was at stake.

He entered the workshop to find Yeshua uncharacteristically listless at his tools, sitting in a stupor. He wore only his long, plain linen shirt and rope belt about his waist, his tallit hung upon the wall. His round face was lifeless as his soft chin stooped toward the ground. Yosef patted his short, curly black hair in greeting. Yeshua made no response, his wine-dark eyes remained locked in place, gazing into an abyss that Yosef could not discern.

The space was rather modest, only a lean-to against their house. Nothing but lattice and layers of palm fronds made for the roof covering, repaired and replaced on a yearly basis.

Many of their projects were difficult to execute. The workshop was longer than it was wide, and it wasn't that long. Whenever they had to spin a timber about, which happened more often than they liked, they had to carry it out of the workshop, serpentine through the narrow courtyard out into the unlevel street, in order to turn around and then carry it back inside along the same meandering, teetering path. The process was as cumbersome as it was heavy. Neighbors called the spectacle "the wooden caterpillar."

It smelled like a carpenter's space. That much never changed. The wood chips and sawdust of many species collected on the ground like a melodious mélange of odors; the air never tasted right to Yosef without the tinge of timbers to it. The carpenter and his apprentice produced craftsmanship of the first order. Their means were limited, but their abilities were boundless.

Yosef had seen the lad lost in thought before, many times, only to emerge from his reverie with a newly refined joinery detail or an improvement to the efficiency of tasks. Even in his stillness, he was active. This particular moment, however, something was very different.

Not knowing what was going on with his son just yet, the kindly father thought to err on the side of courtesy and give his apprentice the decency of a few moments to resume his work. Yosef busied himself with the usual tasks upon return to the workshop. He removed the pronounced chip of cedar that was tucked behind his right ear, the worn item that publicly designated him as a carpenter on days of work, and laid it on his shelf. He took off his cloak and set it upon the hanging hook by the entryway. The carpenter reverently removed his tefillin from his head and left arm, lovingly wound the tiny compartments within their leather straps, then placed them right next to Yeshua's within a small box that had been framed and hung upon the wall against the house.

For a moment Yosef meditated on the mitzvot written upon the small parchments within the tefillin. As a faithful Jew, the father of the messiah regarded the mitzvot not as commandments so much as opportunities to please HaShem through obedience. It was his delight to fulfill a mitzvah several times a day.

He retrieved a tiny palmful of oats and gave it to their only donkey as he petted it behind the ears. Yeshua took to calling him Shimshon, and his father liked the name well enough, as did the rest of the family. It wasn't long before the children were calling the beast Shimmy, although Yosef could never quite bring himself to that nickname. Still, Yosef found the reference endearing; the beast was as strong and irascible as his namesake of that mighty Judge of old.

Yosef had only purchased the creature about a year prior, but what a productive year it had been. The carpenter took all of his responsibilities most seriously, which had come to include training this animal. Many tricks and feats had come into his repertoire. At present, he only wanted for the donkey to move a little further away from his son. At the sound of a few clicks out of the side of one cheek and a gentle nudge from the man, Shimshon sidled over to the far side of the workshop and there sat in contentment, idly munching away at his oats.

Even after Yosef's busying himself all those minutes in the workspace, Yeshua was as unresponsive as when his father had arrived.

"Now, what's this, son of mine? I had figured that you would already have begun dovetailing the king post by now!" Yosef exclaimed.

Yeshua remained motionless, transfixed on the timber before him, staring straight through the thing. Yosef wondered what had come over his boy. Was this the onset of the sullen coming-of-age years they had been told to expect? Nothing was ever normal with him, anyhow. Nothing like his siblings. Nothing like his friends. Good as he was, being his father was an ongoing challenge, more so than with the other children.

"I'm sorry, Abba. I didn't mean to slacken the pace today. I just..." Yeshua stopped.

It was even less like Yeshua to falter in his speech. He either spoke, or he listened, even as a child. What in Heaven's Name had come over him?

Yosef sat next to him on the bench and placed his arm around him. Yeshua was filling out his frame, sinews taut with lean muscle. Nevertheless, the lad was still too young, much too young for the heady things he grappled with. This weight, whatever it might be, was too much for those slender shoulders.

"Would you like to tell me whatever is the matter?" Yosef asked.

"No, Abba... if only for your sake," Yeshua replied.

Yosef looked at the pain in Yeshua's face, heard the heaviness in his breathing, felt the tension in his fists.

"Well, my son, you are clearly disturbed. While I do not enjoy reminding you of this now, we still have much work to finish before the day is done. Would you speak with your father?" Yosef pleaded.

The tears welled up in Yeshua's eyes once again. He steeled himself as if preparing to take a blow to the face, resolute to hang on for dear life. This distress was unlike him.

"Is it another bully?" Yosef pried.

Yeshua shook his head.

"Is it... a girl..?" Yosef prodded.

Again, Yeshua shook his head.

"Are you still upset about the chisel? Because the blacksmith has agreed to..."

It was nearly an outburst when Yeshua blurted, "I received a vision, Abba... of the end of my days! I will die at the hands of Romans and Jews alike, nailed to a timber like this!"

Then he wept bitterly, unrestrained, desperate, like a maniac drowning, frantic, reaching blindly for a rope. The tears flowed freely into his father's chest. Yosef held him tight, a bastion in the storm, full of compassion and alarm all at once. He had learned many things after the episode at the Temple last year. But, by Yerushalayim, he was not prepared for this.

Yosef wondered if his little man had witnessed a crucifixion somehow. He knew that it was inevitable, that he would come to know the horror of such things. Nevertheless, he strove to keep all of his children from growing up too soon in the shadow of a darkened world. The roads they traveled, the schedules they kept. Yosef was strict in his desire to keep his little ones innocent for as long as he possibly could. Few things ever went according to Yosef's plans, all the more so with this particular child.

He wondered how no one from inside the house came to check on them. In the years to come, Yosef could never quite remember how long the wailing went on before they just continued to hold onto each other. For all the violence at the onset of that storm, the eye at its center was all the more tranquil.

Yeshua had come of age according to the traditions of their people, but had anyone ever fostered a messiah before? At what age was the future king supposed to come into the fulness of his maturity? In many ways, Yosef would make things up as they went along and hope to Gan Eden that all would be well. At this moment, however, his duties were abundantly clear. He would become an indomitable granite wall of tenderness. He rocked his son back and forth like he had during his infancy.

As much as Yosef hated the grief in his son's lament, he knew well enough to cherish the preciousness of this space in time, for it would soon depart beyond hope of return. The wings of childhood, once fully fledged, never carried the little soul back home. He would hold onto Yeshua as long as the grief-stricken child clung to him. Whatever the future may hold, this boy was not the messiah yet, by calling perhaps, but not by stature, by no means. At the moment, he was nothing but a frightened thirteen-year-old coming to grips with his uncertain place in an unforgiving world.

An age passed within that embrace.

Gently, Yosef asked, "Come, my son, and tell me true. Did your vision show that this would come to pass soon?"

"No, Abba. In the vision I was full-grown, having come into my own, proclaiming my Father's Kingdom to all Yisrael."

Yosef hesitated a moment. He and Miriam had spent several weeks of restless nights arguing back and forth about the boy's inexplicable behavior last year. Yosef did not understand. He couldn't even pretend to begin to understand. But he would relent. He had learned not to take the "my Father" language personally. Whatever else was at work in Yeshua's mind, otherworldly as that was in itself, Yosef knew that he had the boy's love. Of that much he was certain. He always felt respected and enjoyed by this strange child. And he loved being called Abba... somehow even more especially when Yeshua said it.

Again, Yosef asked, "Well... does it happen with this piece of wood?"

Yeshua chuckled at that, albeit only a little. "No, Abba... this will become a fine rafter with nothing but good dreams and well-wishing affixed to it. That, and my insignia, hidden at the top."

One thing this pious man had learned as the steward of a charge so demanding was never to attempt to argue away the boy's convictions. Once Yeshua had come to certainty about something, there was no changing his mind. He was submissive in his posture all the way through, but his thoughts were his own. Yosef had learned to meet him where he was, wherever that happened to be. Whatever the situation, the father had to inhabit the parameters of Yeshua's expressions if they were going to achieve anything in dialogue. It had long been clear that his son oriented himself to the world only from the ground of his own being when all was said and done.

"That is too bad, then. Assuredly I tell you, my son: if it meant saving you from the thought of such doom, I would have nailed myself to this beam right now and been done with it. Of course, that would have become somewhat difficult to explain to your mother!"

The smile that broke on Yeshua's face glistened beneath the stain of his many tears. Even his short, curly hair seemed less morose. His big, almond-shaped, wine-dark eyes went from baleful to beautiful as he looked full in the face of his father.

"Oh! Abba, how I love you. I have always been so glad that my Father smiled upon me, that I should have been born into your house. You have my heart in full. Truly. But you could no more take my place in this work that is set before me than you could replace Ima in the kitchen!"

Then, tears still wet on his face, Yeshua laughed. The music of his mirth was a great, raucous song that erupted from his belly and shook the sky. Angels' breath – his joy always resounded so free. Sometimes Yosef thought that he heard other voices laughing along in the background of some other room right around the corner.

Yosef laughed as well, and almost as loud. Even for the thick air of sadness, it was too true not to be funny. Yosef had been a master carpenter for many years, but he had never been anything but a miserable cook. No matter how hard he tried, he could never seem to produce anything worthwhile for his time in the kitchen. He so badly wanted to give his wife rest when he could. It took the children's commensurate lack of appetites to put an end to those efforts. Miriam found it endearing, but she wouldn't eat much on those occasions, either.

After all these years and wonders, Yosef still didn't understand the lad. But he had learned two things at least. Despite appearances at times, Yeshua always intended obedience. And sometimes all that he needed was room to grow. Yosef continued to do his very best to give him that much.

"Would you like to go down to the spring, Yeshua?"

"Thank you, Abba, but we have dovetails to finish."

Straightway Yeshua wiped his face, picked up his chisel and mallet, and resumed paring. With the new chisel, Yosef joined him in the work. Every once in a while, the father would steal a glance at his son. Every other once in a while, Yeshua would gift him a brief smile, sincere in its reassurance.

After some time, Yosef rested his hand on Yeshua's shoulder and, half pleading, half insisting,

"Let's make no mention of this to your mother, agreed?" Yosef stressed.

"Amen," said Yeshua.

No matter what manner of misunderstanding might disrupt their relationship, they were never anything but irrevocably united in their love for Miriam. She was often sharing with Yosef some newfound realization about her miracle child as she kept a perfect memory of anything that was ever spoken over him. This development, however, did not belong in her keeping. For the first time in Yosef's married life, he decided to shield Miriam from some of the secrecy as he and Yeshua became exclusive confidantes in this matter. For the second time in Yosef's married life, fidelity had just become more complicated.

They finished their day's labors in a companionable silence. As soon as they could they hastened out of the workshop and rejoined the family at the hearth before sundown. Shabbat was drawing near.

Yosef would carry the pain of his son's grief alone. No one could hear of it. No one. From then on, he would have to guard this new silent conspiracy of two within the already delicate insurrection of a few.

It seemed that HaShem, His Name be praised, had disrupted Yosef's plans once again. This was not the kind of conversation he was supposed to have with his son on this day. Instead of discussing the urgent matters of preparation and training, he found himself consoling his little man about this ludicrous vision of his eventual demise.

This carpenter born of a great line of kings was a truly humble man, with a peaceful tranquility that emanated from his being. However, coming to grips with a revelation such as this rattled him all the way to his bones. It was too much for a father to bear. It was certainly too much for any man to bear alone.

As Yeshua left the workshop and entered the home, Yosef lingered by himself for a moment.

He cast a woeful glance to the sky. And he prayed.

"Our Father, Our King, by the Glory of the Throne, how would Heaven have me to steward a messiah doomed to die? Of all days to give him a vision! Surely, this cannot be the way of things..."

2

The Master's Smithery

YESHUA LOVED TO see the other tradesmen at their work. Knowing this, Yosef took him along on these errands whenever he could. More often than not Yosef needed him to look after the workshop or the household, but he did love these opportunities whenever possible.

For one thing, it was always good to see the boy light up with wonder at the sight of things that mesmerized him. Of course, that could happen any time, in the marketplace, at home, at play – most of all at synagogue. Nevertheless, there was still something else, something special about the way that Yeshua would peer in upon the labors of other craftsmen. Yosef felt like he was giving a gift in time during these outings.

For another, Yosef himself would light up at the sight. He was very good at what he did, a master in every way. His only limitations were those imposed by the space of their workshop as well as the manifold constraints of basic poverty. He was thankful to HaShem for an honorable livelihood, for the ability to provide for his family with skill. Yet it was still a concentrated effort to ward off bitterness at the struggle of it all.

All of that dissipated in the light of Yeshua's face. With him, it was enough to simply watch things as they happened. He looked upon men at work as if they were angels at the Dawn of Creation, laying the plumb lines of the heavens and setting the cornerstones of the foundations of the deep. In the company of his son's countenance, Yosef wondered how much of that likening might be true.

There was something elementally satisfying about the smithy. Everything was both familiar and entirely different all at once. The familiarity was in the commonality of the trades. The devices and the creations were different, but the basic rigorousness and craftsmanship were the same. Men always resonate with the essence of masculinity, whatever its means of expression.

More than anything else, the smell of the place was incomparable. It was strange to find something so acrid at the same time so satisfying. Carpentry was rife with many smells, each process and species of wood bequeathing distinct gifts to olfaction. Blacksmithing, however, was more static. The dinginess never changed. And even for that weight of dirtiness in the air, it was impossible not to be invigorated by its odor. The working of iron wrought something all its own within the fires of a man's blood.

Today, however, Yosef wished so badly that he had not taken Yeshua along. This was supposed to have been a simple errand: pay for the chisel, discuss the pergola, move along. Alas, it was not to be.

"What do you mean the chisel costs twice as much as last time?! I know better than that, Shlomo. They have not increased the taxes on us nearly that much, not by far!"

Shlomo was a barrel-chested wall of a man. Yosef was not a diminutive man by any means, but he looked it next to Shlomo, who was bigger-boned and thicker-skinned by nature. Blacksmithing added another dimension of burliness to his already sturdy frame. His brow was as stout as an anvil with ears that could hang hammers. His cheeks were that of a man that smiled and laughed both loud and often. As for his beard, Yosef could never make sense of how it was wider than it was long, as if any hair below his chin was only there as a result of having grown down from his cheeks. Most of the time, he was pleasant enough to be around. Sometimes, however, his smile came with an unpleasant agenda.

"Ah, but Yosef, you are not taking into account the price of the metal itself..."

Yeshua had looked upon their disagreement for at least ten minutes, which is quite a long time when men argue in a fluster. Well, Yosef was flustered. Shlomo seemed to be enjoying himself. He was quite relaxed as he stroked the grungy hair on his thick forearms.

"Stop right there, Shlomo, don't try that either! You forget that I am privy to the metal market myself, purchasing various implements in my trade, too. Although I work in wood, I work with metal as well. Do not try to take me for a simpleton in your deceit!"

"Moshe's beard, Yosef! Hold a minute, brother. An accusation like that would require another witness, would it not? Unless you only mean to hurt my feelings. Then I must tell you that you have succeeded. I hoped that you would have thought better of me than that..."

"Enough, Shlomo, I don't have time..."

"Please, Yosef, restrain yourself. I wouldn't want you to go and say something else unwarranted. It is only the two of us here, after all. Do you suppose that we will require an arbiter to settle the matter?"

It was a brilliant stroke. Even though Shlomo was rude to disregard Yeshua standing right there with them, Yosef could see that he was trapped. No one had witnessed their previous conversation. At the same time, he was realizing how this was Shlomo's intention from the beginning, to play the generous friend days ago, selling the tool on credit, only to hike the price once the payment was delivered. And Yosef had to admit it, even if only to himself: they had never formally agreed on a price. It was Yosef's unassuming nature that sprung the trap.

"Fine, Shlomo. Please explain to me exactly how it is that this chisel came to cost twice as much as the last one that I purchased from you."

"Oh, Yosef, gladly, my friend, gladly! In fact, as we have been deliberating between ourselves, I have realized that it's slightly more than double. You see, that particular chisel was forged with more attention to detail than the last one...”

“It looks exactly the same as the last one! Aside from being broken, they are identical!”

“Yosef, please, allow me to speak. Didn’t you ask me a question concerning its composition?”

Now it had become just plain shameful. Shlomo was actively swindling Yosef, yet he managed to muster the chutzpah to play the rabbi while he was at it. The man could style himself as one walking the high road even in the middle of a sham. It was sham-full.

The two men were elders together in their synagogue. For Yosef, it was unthinkable to take advantage of another man simply because he could drive a wedge into the opening. That they were fellow Jews made the issue even more unconscionable. For Shlomo, it was simply business. Yosef had to reckon with the plain fact that conscience would not be his ally in this negotiation.

“Continue,” said Yosef through gritted teeth (and clenched fists).

“Thank you, Yosef, thank you. As I was saying, that particular chisel was forged with more attention to detail than the last one – on the inside!”

Shlomo paused, as if expecting another outburst from Yosef. But it seemed that Yosef had finally learned his lesson about interrupting an opportunist. It was hard to beat a man at his own game.

Shlomo continued in style. “Blacksmithing is difficult work, Yosef, and not for the faint of heart. The process is excruciating. And while the common eye cannot tell, some of the instruments are beaten twice as much in the process of forging as others. I don’t want to bore you with the many details, and, truth be told, I can’t exactly teach you everything about a blacksmith’s skill set in a single day. Suffice it to say that the tool in discussion represents twice as much blacksmithing as before, if not more. Of course, it isn’t that I made something slipshod the first time. I simply sold you something more economical, initially. Then, when you came to me with a broken chisel, I knew right then that I had to supply you with the very best, capable of surviving the accidental abuses of an apprentice."

He said that last bit with a wink and a laugh as he mussed Yeshua's hair and clapped him on the back. And Yeshua smiled. He actually smiled back at the man! Then Yosef realized that Yeshua had been grinning the whole time. The argument had not deterred his joy whatsoever. At first, he had thought that it was only the surroundings of the smithy that had Yeshua somewhat absentminded in his delight. But no. It angered Yosef to realize that Yeshua also found this exchange amusing. Yosef felt betrayed.

While Shlomo tried to get the boy to speak up, to say something, anything, Yosef took a moment to calm himself. He couldn't exactly leave the back-and-forth and walk out his aggression. That would have given his opponent far too much ground upon his return. And the blacksmith had already won. Were there any means left to rally?

As he looked around the smithy, Yosef found himself beginning to reenter that innocent delight he saw on his son's face. When he allowed himself to be simply present, he just loved the environment. Everything was inherently masculine. The tools, the forge itself, the crucible, the arrangement of space. The entire atmosphere satisfied the whole soul at a glance, to be able to take in at a single setting the complete process of the creation of enduring contraptions. Blacksmithing might be the only trade that provided this panoramic mirror for the soul.

Yosef tempered himself in patience and took several breaths in that one thought. All of them here in this room, in this forge, were still being made. And this argument, as unwelcome as it was, to be taken advantage of by a friend and fellow Jew, was a part of the process, too.

The worst part of it all was wondering what Yeshua thought of him presently, as all fathers yearn more than anything for their sons' admiration as well as their daughters' adoration. Was Yeshua proud of his father for controlling his temper? Was he ashamed of him for being played so handily? Yosef dared not look at his son to find out, not yet.

Yosef did not know what he would do for their month's provisions once he had paid Shlomo's price, whatever that amounted to. But he remembered how many worse plights HaShem had brought his family through already. Heaven's Abode – the very existence of his family was founded upon miracles. They had escaped the destruction of madmen before, stealing across nations to do so. This room and its petty manipulator were small things to navigate. Yosef would relent.

He looked around the smithy again, this time disburdened; he saw the story in the process anew. Yosef would trust in the Master's Craft, in the hand that wielded them all in gentleness. He would trust that he was in the care of HaShem.

And then he saw it, the stack of timbers arranged neatly to the side storage. After his chagrin, he grinned a quiet little grin within. An idea had set in.

"All right, Shlomo. I see now the error of my ways. How much will it be?" Yosef asked, polite as a first-time buyer.

Shlomo had feigned at tinkering as Yosef gathered his wits. He knew that he had the advantage, it was just a matter of waiting for the smelting to cool. Even though he was slightly taken aback by the sudden change in Yosef's tone, it was not nearly enough to be deterred from his purpose. He stated the price, somewhat more than double the usual amount, and Yosef paid the full sum right away. That exchange nearly emptied his purse.

As it was, Yosef did not seem deflated anymore. When he turned the dealings to another matter the next moment, he seemed as strong in his lungs as the bellows that Shlomo would return to using in a little while.

"Do I see the pergola's cedar over there, my friend?" Yosef asked, still as warm as a summer rain.

Shlomo's face beamed and his chest swelled just a little.

"Indeed you do, you fine carpenter, you! It is still a surprise to her, she knows nothing of the project, but my wife will be elated once you have finished it. That is, if you are still eager to do the building for us..?" The blacksmith never missed an opportunity to condescend.

The pergola construction would be good work. That much was true. However, this chisel haggling nearly wiped out any potential profit from the build. Yosef could tell now that the blacksmith had calculated the precise amount that he could extort without running Yosef and his family straight into starvation. One had to admit, there was a cunning to his treachery.

"Of course, of course, Shlomo. Let us put this recent misunderstanding behind us. It was my fault, after all. Who am I to tell a blacksmith his business? I should have known better than to leave the smithy of a man such as yourself without knowing, with certainty, the terms of our agreement."

Shlomo could hear the forehanded insult and the backhanded compliment alike in Yosef's admission. But he was still on the winning side of the exchange, so it didn't upset him in the least. Having won handily, Yosef's subtle remonstrations were only a couple of gnats to swat away.

"Ah, speak nothing of it, my friend, nothing of it at all. It's only smoke through the chimney. Anyhow, we have come through worse together, haven't we?" Shlomo said this with a heavy-handed slap on the back.

Yosef tilted forward a bit at the gesture, recovering his balance. He also found himself wondering what that "worse" occasion could have been. Come to think of it, he wondered if they had seen better together, too.

"Indeed, brother, indeed. We sons of Avraham have suffered many things over the ages. And we are still here, are we not?"

"Amen and amen! We are still here! HaShem be praised!"

The blacksmith never missed an opportunity for exuberance, either.

"HaShem be praised," Yosef echoed. "Shall we discuss the pergola, then? Do you have the same construction in mind as we drew up last time?"

"Absolutely, Yosef, no changes at all – except for the wood itself. No offense, but I suspected that I might be able to acquire a better load of cedar than you happened to have on hand. HaShem smiled on me with the find."

"No offense taken, Shlomo. No offense at all. A man of your means is capable of a great many things. Do you mind if I look the lot over?"

Shlomo inclined with a grand gesture of welcome. It was showing off, of course. Yosef didn't seem to mind.

Yosef knew better than to think that happenstance was at work here. It had nothing whatsoever to do with a better load but a better price, perhaps no price at all. This was Shlomo, after all. Some other poor soul was hoodwinked in that exchange. In any event, Yosef was astute enough to recognize a twist of fate when he saw it. It was about time that Shlomo received the treatment of his own trickery for a change.

"Do you know where the cedar was sourced?" Yosef asked. He stroked the timbers studiously and rapped upon them a few times as if awaiting a response.

"Only that I got it through one of your competitors, my friend. It must be Lebanese, you know. Is it to your liking, Yosef?"

"It is. This wood will shape beautifully in my hands. Are you still insistent that I do this without my son's assistance?"

"Now, Yosef, I mean no offense to your apprentice here, or to your training for that matter. I simply want it to be said that the structure was built exclusively by the hands of the master."

The blacksmith never missed an opportunity for grandiloquence, as it turned out.

Yeshua didn't seem to take any offense at having been slighted. He continued to wear that boyish grin, unfazed by any of the dickering.

Yosef wondered how much the boy took in at moments like these. Come what may, he knew that some question from the event would come back to haunt him somewhere down the road.

"That's fine, Shlomo. We will make do. That is what we are best at, isn't it, Yeshua?"

Yeshua spoke up for the first time since being in the smithy, still smiling wide.

"Very much so, Abba!"

Even in that instant, Shlomo looked pleased with himself that he had some hand in a teachable father-son moment.

"The only concern that I have," mused Yosef, "is the age of the wood. It looks to be twice as old as the cedar that I had on hand last month." Yosef stroked his beard as if struck with a dilemma. "Your anniversary is next month, is it not?"

"It is," said Shlomo, sounding suspicious for the first time that day.

"Therein lies our problem, brother. This cedar being as old as it is, it will take me twice as long to make the mortises and tenons, not to mention planing it down for the elegant likings of your lovely wife. I'm afraid a month won't be enough time."

"What does the age of the wood have to do with the carpentry, Yosef?!" asked Shlomo incredulously.

"Well, my friend, the growth rings are twice as many! The wood has double the density. The wear and tear it plays upon the tools, the fatigue it causes in the hands. Look, Shlomo, I don't want to bore you with the many details, and, truth be told, I can't exactly teach you everything about a carpenter's skill set in a single day. Suffice it to say that the wood in discussion represents twice as much carpentry as before, if not more."

And then Yosef could not help himself. He stole a glance in Yeshua's direction to find the boy positively beside himself with glee. Yosef could see that he was trying to contain it, but he was right on the brink of one of his laughing fits.

Yosef thought to himself, as loud as he possibly could, "Hold your peace, boy! Do not ruin this!"

Shlomo was red in the face, stuck in between the hammer and the anvil. It was satisfying to see his bluster beaten down a bit. Yosef couldn't recall if he had ever witnessed the likes except with his wife Tamar.

"Would you like to deal with my competitors that you mentioned? Perhaps they would be able to meet the deadline in time, having at least another master carpenter on hand, you know."

Yosef knew many things about his community, none the least of which included whatever affected his livelihood. He was the only carpenter not engaged in building the Praetor's bathhouse in Sepphoris, right across the valley from Natzeret. Shlomo had no other option than to deal with Yosef, at least if he still wanted to surprise his wife and throw a grand party in time for their twentieth anniversary.

Truth be told, Yosef didn't much love the idea of building a pergola, not initially, but he could find no real conscientious objection to the matter other than its Roman origins. Merely as a woodworker, he had to admit, he liked them well enough. He even had some improvements in mind once he no longer objected to the notion. Now, however, his conscience was completely free. Having the mallet of this moment in hand, he would not soon release it from his grasp.

It turned out that Shlomo also knew Yosef would be his only option, as Yosef suspected he might (Yosef also suspected that he was the object of Shlomo's best haggling). The real problem was that the blacksmith did not like being dealt with in this manner. Shlomo was not accustomed to being spun about in his dealings. He would sooner have no deal at all than a deal at a disadvantage.

"Perhaps my wife and I will travel instead," Shlomo harrumphed. "I can offload the cedar before then and recoup my losses."

"Oh, and well you should," Yosef sympathized. "What is of utmost importance is that your lovely lady would feel celebrated on your special day. That much is clear. And I am pretty certain that Miriam made no mention of the pergola to your wife, anyway..."

"Wait, are you saying..?" Shlomo worried.

"Well, I can't be absolutely certain, Shlomo. I mean, it never occurred to me to ask Miriam if she had mentioned it to Tamar. Miriam is usually so discreet. It wouldn't be like her to go about gabbing something like that. Still, you know how it is whenever wives get to talking. Maybe it came up? But traveling sounds lovely, too. Where do you think you might go?"

Yosef knew enough about Shlomo and Tamar, as did everyone in the community. The brute was a force of nature with everyone except his wife. He may have been the head of the house, but she was the crown upon his head, one that he constantly strove to keep balanced. Shlomo would not do anything to disturb her place of prestige and entitlement within their home. The seed of doubt was just enough to stop Shlomo in his tracks. If there were any chance that she had caught wind of the pergola, the blacksmith was sunk. All that Yosef had to do was to knock in the final pegs.

As Shlomo was frozen with indecision, fuming silently, Yosef proposed a solution.

"You know, if you wanted to move forward with the project, I think that we could manage to build the pergola in time for your anniversary party. I would simply need the help of my apprentice to satisfy the deadline. And I will tell you true, he has become a little master himself. The only thing between Yeshua and that designation is a believable age. You could retain that boast that you so desire (and the compliment to me, thank you). What's more, you would still get your pergola in time, Shlomo. That is, of course, if you even want to move forward with it."

Shlomo hesitated ever so slightly. He was keen to moments when the upper hand changed during a negotiation. He would not allow his assailant to hoist a heavier hammer and make things worse. Or so he thought.

"Fine," Shlomo grumbled. He retrieved the sum of money that Yosef had paid him minutes earlier, plus a little more. It worked out to the amount of their original agreement, the one with the "younger" cedar.

"What's this, Shlomo?" asked Yosef, as innocently as a child seeing a rainbow for the first time. He received the money in hand as if he didn't know what to do with it.

"That's the deposit..."

"Oh, splendid! It will be beautiful, and your wife will love it. Of that I have no doubt. But, you know, my friend, I customarily take a fifty percent deposit before beginning the work. And this..."

"...Should be more than enough!" Shlomo interrupted. "I have the cedar right here!"

"Too true, brother, too true," Yosef soothed. "However, you must remember that, even though the little master will be working with me during the project, now that you have agreed so graciously, I myself will have to work twice as hard. Skilled as he is, he isn't a full-grown man just yet. I am still more vigorous for the time being. Sometimes age has its benefits, no?"

Shlomo muttered something unintelligible as he handed over the hefty increase, nearly thrusting it into Yosef's chest. He had lost any semblance of hospitality. He nodded at the pile of timbers as if he might head-butt them when he spat out, "All right, then! Now I must get back to my work and let you get started on yours!"

"Quite right, Shlomo. We will be right on our way. There is only the matter of lost wages that will occur as a result of working exclusively on your pergola. I have already collected those deposits from other customers. Now that Yeshua will not be fulfilling those orders in my stead, I will have to return them."

Yosef looked down at his purse and counted the total, twice.

"This much again should cover it." This time, Yosef spoke without a smile. His face was as set as a scarf joint.

Shlomo had to retrieve the doubled amount from his workbench.

He was flummoxed beyond all hope and humor on the way there and back. He may or may not have dropped the money at Yosef's feet when he returned. Yosef may or may not have minded stooping over to pick the purse up off the floor.

When Yosef stood back up, he reached out to shake Shlomo's hand to seal the deal, which Shlomo grabbed as quickly as he could. Then Shlomo squeezed more than was customary. He was a blacksmith, and a big man, with a mighty grip. But Yosef had a fine carpenter's grip himself. He squeezed back. Neither man lost any face in that handshake, which is to say, Shlomo didn't win any back.

Before he released his grasp, Yosef leaned in and said, "I'll collect the remaining fifty percent upon delivery, brother." For a man that was characteristically so warm, it was all the more eerie when he spoke in ice.

Before Shlomo could protest, or worse, Yosef put their hands down and addressed his son.

"Yeshua, would you be so good as to remind your father of the terms of our agreement when the time comes? I wouldn't want to accidentally extort our friend. Here, you hold the purse and count it all out again, won't you? Let's make for certain that we are all of one mind and memory on this occasion. He is thirteen after all, Shlomo. He will suffice as our witness. Or would you prefer that I bring one of the other elders into our agreement? It's entirely up to you."

There was just the briefest flash of murder that skittered across Shlomo's scowl, but it passed.

"All is well, Yosef. We are agreed." Then he turned his back on them and returned to the forge.

Yosef and Yeshua remained motionless for an instant, watching the blacksmith return to his place of power. Then, before anything else might get flung, they turned on their heels. Yosef hollered over his shoulder as they walked away, "I'll come back with the donkey this evening to collect the cedar, Shlomo!"

There was no response except for the angry pinging of a sullen hammer. Yosef wasn't sure what he might be striking. The forge had gone cold long ago.

As they left the smithy and made their way back to the main thoroughfare, they hiked up their garments to make the clamoring descent back home. Shlomo dwelt at the summit of Natzeret, further from the spring at the base but nearer to the fields and vineyards. Every residence in the town involved several trade-offs of one proximity versus another.

Yosef took a deep breath that had been minutes in the waiting. He had calmed himself back in the smithy, but he didn't begin to relax until they left. He did not enjoy tension whatsoever. But he enjoyed being extorted even less, especially at the expense of his family.

Yeshua handed the purse back to his father as they walked. When Yosef took it in hand, he noticed that Yeshua was grinning even more than before, eyes wide with unabashed delight. Then he began to chuckle. Yosef knew where that was going.

"Would you stop laughing like an idiot?" Yosef insisted. He was trying to hide his own smirk in his beard.

"Yes, Abba," said Yeshua. But he only stopped chuckling. That wide, careless smile remained.

"Well..!?" demanded Yosef.

"I'm sorry, Abba. Would you like me to stop grinning, too?"

If it were even possible, Yeshua smiled all the wider. He even squeaked a little as he asked.

Yosef was undone. He chuckled himself, which allowed Yeshua to chuckle again. Then he laughed, and of course Yeshua laughed, too. In a few breaths, they were both laughing like idiots, heedless of their fellow pedestrians on the steep stony streets. Had Yeshua been a full-grown man rather than a lanky looking thirteen-year-old, everyone would have thought them drunk in the middle of the day. As it was, they were a curious spectacle to behold – a very loud, curious spectacle. Yosef relented his concerns. They were out of ear-shot of the smithy by now. At least, he was pretty sure that they were.

With such a generous sum of money in hand, they made several unplanned stops on the way back. The butcher, the baker, a garment vendor. Every time they caught their breath and calmed themselves, Yeshua would stoke the coals all over again.

"Be careful, Abba, the thread count in that blanket is double the normal amount!"

"Abba, check again, that pomegranate looks twice as tasty as usual!"

"Oh no, Abba! The bones in this steak are doubly dense!"

Each and every time, the uproar went on unchecked and without delay between the two. None of the other market-goers had any idea what was so funny, but that didn't stop some of them from laughing along. Between father and son, the joke never got old. At times, all it took was a look to set them off into another silent evocation of reckless giggles. Any time they received a new batch of cedar timbers, one sidelong gander and an eyebrow waggle was enough to deliver the punchline.

They laughed like idiots all the way home.

3

The Houses of Study

YOSEF SNAPPED HIMSELF back from drifting away in his imagination. He glanced at Miriam next to him on his left, their three youngest children beside her, Ya'akov, Yose and their sister, Shlomit. The good father smiled to himself seeing their little feet dangling and swinging beneath their seats. The children were fidgety, but they behaved. Yeshua was the eldest by six years. Most of the young children of the other families played outside the synagogue.

As discreetly as he could, Yosef looked over at Yeshua seated beside him to his right. The boy sat as he always did in this place, unbroken in his focus upon the teaching of Torah. Even in such a commonplace moment as sitting at attention, Yosef wondered at Yeshua's verve. It didn't matter that they were motionless. There was lightning in his son's posture, a quickening in the radiant energy of his frame. To capture such alacrity with not even a word could be unnerving to others at times. However, to the kindly, knowing eyes of Yosef, the father of the messiah, Yeshua was simply full of life.

He had memorized the entirety of the Torah years ago along with the other boys in the synagogue. For all Yosef knew, Yeshua may even have memorized the Prophets and Writings already. He had not asked that question of his son in some while.

Nevertheless, even with the Scriptures buried deep within himself, Yeshua was like a night watchman upon the walls of the City, ever alert, looking forward unto dawn. The boy gave his attention to everything that required it, and he gifted his countenance to anyone that was before him. But nothing captivated him like the study of Torah. If it was ever anything like work to him, then it must have been like the endeavor of a treasure hunt, filled with anticipation and excitement at every step, because he never tired of it.

The men had spent a tireless year in the assembly of the synagogue, committing nearly all of their evenings and many sacrificial days to its erection. Theirs was a community abounding with craftsmen. All requisite skills were in ample supply between fathers and sons. They wanted for nothing in talent. And they never lacked a full minyan of ten men in attendance daily.

The source of their endowments was conflicting for Yosef. Their synagogue had an entire wing devoted to the assembly of the God-fearers in their company. Most of the communities had made what space they could for the Gentiles that were intrigued with Torah, but very few had done so as much as Yosef's community had. This was due in no small part to their centurion benefactor, Gaius, their greatest contributor of material wealth in the dedication of the synagogue.

Despite the relative smallness of Natzeret, they attracted several God-fearers from the neighboring city of Sepphoris. Herod's city possessed great wealth, but Natzeret was rich in its studies. Even the Gentiles could acknowledge the difference between the substance of teachings.

The reconciliation of opposing impulses remained an ongoing dilemma for the father of the messiah. In truth, he was grateful for such opulence as was before them. Had they not had the benefaction of the centurion, and his reverent peering into the Torah and the God of Yisrael, they would not have so much as half of the study materials that they had in their possession. As it was, they had amassed the entirety of the Scriptures, so that all of the Torah and the Prophets were ever before them, available to all qualified to handle with care and proper training. They even possessed the extant Wisdom

Literature, while the nation's Torah-scholars continued to debate which Writings were authoritative. Very few communities could make such claims throughout all of Yisrael.

Yosef looked around him at the awesome display of his community's capabilities. There was only one grand entrance, double doors set on massive hinges with copperwork filigree set into spiraling staircase reliefs within the slabs. Windows ringed the synagogue and the casements were ornate with inscriptions from the Torah and Prophets. Molding along the ceiling had been set in plaster in the imitation of grapevines. The entire floor work was an extravagant mosaic depicting two vast bronze doors set into ironwork hinges as if they led to a subterranean vault beneath the synagogue.

The carpenter admired the bimah at the forefront that he had been entrusted to fashion, the sacred place from which the holy scrolls were read. It was both mighty and meticulous in its construction. Yosef had hewn it from a whole tree trunk, cut to the height of a man's chest and sprawling the width of four men side-by-side. Although it was one monolithic piece, it looked like a tabletop set within the branches of a tree as though the podium had grown up from the ground and they had built the synagogue around it. It took a dozen men and a team of donkeys an entire day to move the immense monument into place.

It was inevitable. Every time Yosef appreciated the craftsmanship of their synagogue, he would find his eyes turning toward Gaius across the way. Without fail, the commanding centurion would sense Yosef's gaze and respond in kind. There wasn't much of a protocol for such moments. The two men shared a room but they were divided by entire worlds. Their recognition of each other would always end with a measured, mutual nod, as surreptitious as it was respectful.

On this day, the teacher stood at the bimah and read from the final writings of Moshe, a portion from Devarim, in the section where the Prophet taught about what is permissible in divorce. According to the schedule of readings in the synagogues, this passage was a matter of focused discussion every year. Whenever it came back around to this portion, no one ever enjoyed it.

Rabbi Nechemyah presided over the service. He was a student in the House of Hillel, one of the greatest masters of Torah that Yisrael would ever know. The sage was old, thin and lively. He was a tall man. His wispy gray hair had thinned with age and his face was etched with the travails of all his years. He had been a coal-maker by trade and he had clever fingers. His prevailing idiosyncrasy was to blink constantly. Yosef could never determine whether that had to do with his manner of thinking or if it had become an ingrained reflex of working with soot. The man was unstoppably blunt with the adults but he was magnanimous with the children. They all loved him.

"'When a man takes a wife and marries her, then it shall be, if she finds no favor in his eyes because he has found some unseemly thing in her, that he shall write her a certificate of divorce, put it in her hand, and send her out of his house.' Hear the Torah of Moshe!" the teacher pronounced at the end of his reading.

The congregation returned their "amen" as was proper during the liturgy. However, the discomfort of the room was palpable. Husbands were shrewd in their slowness to engage the deliberation. If anyone were to avail themselves of their legal liberties in divorce, the proceedings were no easy matter. To simply speak of the issue, even as an intellectual exercise of curiosity, could work all kinds of contention within one's household for the following week, if not much longer. The gathering remained uncharacteristically quiet in their private ruminations alongside one another.

Yet here Yeshua sat, ebullient as always before Torah. Normally, he was required to bide his time for an opportunity to join the discussion, giving preference to the older men. On many Shabbat gatherings he had no chance to interject, with other privileged voices filling up the time. On this day, however, no one joined in the fray. Calculated hesitation became the apparent rule.

Before the teacher might proceed with the liturgy, Yeshua asked him,

"Rabbi, what should we learn from this teaching?"

Yosef breathed in just a little too sharp, in part because he had hoped that his son might stay out of this one, in part because Miriam had clutched his arm with both hands as soon as Yeshua spoke aloud.

"Ah! A question from our budding Torah teacher!" the sage acknowledged him.

"We always look forward to the reflections of our wonder-boy here, don't we, brothers and sisters?"

"Amen!" The congregation chuckled at that.

"He fills us all with wonder, Rabbi, even his own parents!" Shlomo bellowed. "They might spend three whole days wondering where he could be!" The blacksmith spared no volume, as he always made sure that his quips rang out clear as an anvil strike.

Everyone laughed all the louder, even the closest friends of Yosef and Miriam, try as they might to restrain themselves. They never stood a chance of living down the Temple misadventure from their last Pesach festival.

Yosef feigned a smile and played along with the joke, nodding dejectedly and surrendering a single hand in the air. Miriam continued to forcibly detain his nearest arm. She gave no pretense to saving face.

Through it all, Yeshua grinned well enough at himself for the jest, although he held the teacher in his gaze.

The sage gently waved his arms before the gathering, calling for a hush. As many in attendance either wiped the tears from their eyes or cleared the sniggers from their throats, Nechemyah swallowed his own grin before he responded at last.

"What mystery sets itself before you, child of wonder? Is the writing unclear in what manner a man might divorce his wife?"

"The surface is quite clear, Teacher. Nevertheless, are there no depths for us to plunge with this portion of the Scroll unrolled before us?" Yeshua returned.

"Indeed, child, indeed." Nechemyah brightened. "Surely you will learn for yourself someday that marriage is a many-eddied spring of waters, sometimes bitter, sometimes sweet."

Husbands and wives chuckled alike as knowing nods and glances bounded about the room. Perhaps a few elbows were exchanged at chuckles and nods deemed too emphatic.

"Do you think, Yeshua, that we might cause the bitter water to spring forth if we strike the text too hard?" It was a veiled plea from the teacher that Yeshua would relent. Truly, Nechemyah loved his people, and he was wise enough to know the difficulties fraught in this discussion.

However, Yeshua was relentless. Yosef wondered if he might be naïve to the dangers of proceeding, even as he remembered how perceptive his son always was to the inner workings of hearts and minds. Yeshua usually concealed his thoughts, but occasionally Yosef was privileged to them. The boy was no dolt when it came to people, no matter how strangely they might perceive him.

"Amen, Teacher. We might indeed. So, shall we not whisper our way through the Words instead, and bring forth the sweet waters? As it is written, 'on His Torah he meditates day and night. He will be like a tree planted by the streams of water.'"

Once again, and not for the last time, Yosef marveled at Yeshua's ability to call the calamity of a crowd into a calm of contemplation. Only moments ago, the boy was the laughing stock of the room. In a single instant, he had everyone peering into the Teachings of HaShem in the quiet worship of study. The very word "whisper" on his son's lips brought a thunderous stillness to the room.

"Let it be so, Yeshua. Amen. As it is written, 'Behold, these are but the outskirts of his ways; how small a whisper do we hear of Him!' Nevertheless, as the text continues, 'But the thunder of His power who can understand?'"

The sage had finally acknowledged the validity of Yeshua's question even as he called for caution. Nechemyah sat down away from the bimah as he proceeded to teach.

"Amen, teacher," Yeshua agreed. "May we in our study ascend with David? 'My heart is not proud, nor my eyes lofty, nor do I concern myself with great matters, or things too wonderful for me. Surely I have stilled and quieted my soul.'"

"Very well, child," Nechemyah continued. "How many ways do you consider that a man might find disfavor with his wife? For even the Wise did not presume to understand these mysteries. 'Three things are too wonderful for me, four I do not understand: the way of an eagle in the air, the way of a serpent upon a rock, the way of a ship in the middle of the sea, and the way of a man with a maiden.'"

Yeshua answered. "Surely, they are many, but isn't joy meant to reside there? 'Rejoice in the wife of your youth.'"

"So it should be. And what should a man do whenever joy does not reside there," Nechemyah asked, "when 'continual dripping on a rainy day and a contentious wife are alike?'"

Yosef could not help but wonder if his son would be outclassed by the sage in this debate. After all, Yeshua was only thirteen, too young to be married. Nechemyah had real life experience behind the weight of his exegesis. Even if Yeshua somehow managed to win the exchange, he might lose the audience. The father of the messiah knew well enough that public opinion was more winsome than truth alone. However, Yosef had little time to wonder about his son's fate, as he soon found himself wincing at the whiplash crack of quick wit that Yeshua leveled at their teacher.

"Should we consider the husband blameless when he finds himself with such a wife? Since we are told that 'through laziness the roof sinks in; and through idleness of the hands the house leaks,'" Yeshua rejoined.

At that, the synagogue became full of hooping, hollering and all manner of uproar. Several husbands stood up in defiance as if they had just been personally accused of neglecting their households. Wives clucked in approval, chiding their men with the list of unfulfilled chores and errands. More than a few congregants did in fact have leaking roofs at the time of their gathering. The metaphor may have been lost on many, but the effect was successful nevertheless.

Yosef and Miriam did not so much as stir in their seats. It was at this time that Yosef became acutely aware of a sensation in his arm that had passed on from discomfort and further along right into pain. When he attempted to pull his right arm toward his center to rub at it, he found it still inside Miriam's clutches, her nails having been dug into his forearm for longer than he knew. He would not be getting his arm back to himself any time soon. So, he placed his left hand on top of Miriam's grip... and she relaxed her squeeze... even if only a little.

All the while, Yeshua kept his steady gaze fixed on Nechemyah, heedless of the hullabaloo about him, unresponsive to anyone calling him to account. One might have thought him placid save for the indefatigable light in his wine-dark eyes. This was no passive student. Neither was he impertinent. He was too reverent, too delighted in the interplay of Torah for any of that.

"Well played, Yeshua, well played!" The sage said, his entire face at work propping up his wispy eyebrows.

Despite his initial reticence, Nechemyah was excited by the debate. It wouldn't be fair to say that he had become unconcerned with the fate of the flock, but Yeshua had managed to bring the Torah-teacher into the enthusiast's space of exegetical frenzy. Scripture was always speaking to Scripture, and no part of the Oracles of HaShem was disconnected from any other. Yeshua's stroke was a masterful parry. He met the familial architecture in the exchange with a deftly applied text speaking within the same metaphor. Nechemyah was engaging a peer all of a sudden. He was having fun and he was not soon to be outdone.

"Would you say that only the husband causes a leaky roof in his own household? For 'every wise woman builds her house, but the foolish one tears it down with her own hands.'"

With that proverb from the sage, the assembled Jews had come into absolute suspense. In one moment, divorce was the husband's fault entirely, in the next it was the wife's. For the time being, no one knew what to think for themselves. They were standing witness to a sparring match between intellectual giants. All that they could do was try to hang on for whatever remained. One thing was certain, this was no laughing matter any longer. Indeed, no one was laughing anymore. Even Shlomo leaned forward in his seat, holding his wife's hand to his barreled chest with hope and desperation in tandem.

Then Yosef realized that riveting as the session had become, he wasn't exactly sure where Yeshua was going with his line of inquiry, which was concurrent to his exegesis. Nechemyah's teaching was standard Pharisaism. That much was clear. The text allowed for divorce over virtually any displeasure whatsoever, and the Pharisees considered themselves faithful to the text.

Yosef knew, absolutely, that Yeshua revered the Torah above all else. As vigorous as he was, even as a child he preferred study over play. Miriam used to limit his time in the synagogue, worried that he would grow up too bookish for his own good. Yeshua was happy to obey, as he always had been. It took years for Yosef to realize that even when Yeshua was playing with other children, he would often sub-vocalize entire scrolls of the Torah and Prophets to himself from memory.

So, Yosef wasn't worried that his son would say something shameful, something unfounded in the Scriptures. Yeshua always had several texts in mind for anything that he stated, whether the conversation was specifically having to do with Torah study or not. Still, this deliberation with the sage could only be troubling. This was a thirteen-year-old boy wading into the weighty dialogue of marriage, after all. What was he thinking?

"Surely, Rabbi," Yeshua responded, "these matters are beyond my own youthful understanding."

Yosef was surprised to hear Yeshua concede the issue so soon. He felt a strange mixture of relief and disappointment. Then, right as Nechemyah's face alighted with a thinly veiled victory, Yeshua continued his thought. Everyone, including Yosef and Miriam, had confused Yeshua's brief concession with final surrender. Dread and excitement overtook Yosef all over again.

"Even the King's mother poses the question, 'Who can find a worthy woman?' As if to say that one does not merely find such a lady... unless he also builds her up. Therefore, we also read, 'By wisdom a house is built; by understanding it is established.'"

For the first time since Yeshua first spoke up, Miriam looked directly into Yosef's face. Yosef knew better than to pretend he didn't notice. He met her countenance with his own, only to find that he could not discern whatsoever the emotional state of his wife.

One of the ongoing problems that Yosef endured in his life with Miriam was just how enticed he was by her! After all their years and trials together, he had never become less attracted to her, only ever more so as their love for one another continued to deepen and refine. It seemed a silly thing to consider as a problem, but it was a difficult complication during arguments. The carpenter was intoxicated by the beauty of his wife. Accordingly, he could not always keep his wits.

Her hair was covered, as it always was whenever they were in public. All of the Pharisees' wives maintained the custom. Nevertheless, even when her glory had been concealed, it only took a look from Miriam, whatever her emotions at the time, to undo Yosef in his resilience. He couldn't help but appreciate her style, the way she dressed the fabric around her head, gliding down her back, with the tail ends drawn out like a waterfall.

Remembering their years in Alexandria, Yosef saw the depths and wonders of the Great Sea when he looked into Miriam's eyes. Her skin was as soft and colorful as those shorelines. Yosef knew her to be ferocious and he just as obsessively thought her to be beautiful. Miriam's gaze penetrated him, beckoned him, terrified him, wooed him. It was an easy matter for him to think upon his wife whenever he reflected on the Song of Songs.

To his eyes, at the moment, she simply looked wild. Whether this would prove good or bad when they returned home, he couldn't say just yet. With the wisdom of Hillel, Yosef kept his face neutral and his manners pleasant. He would not deliberately elicit either a purr or a growl from this tigress seated beside him. Discretion advised him to let her prowl on her own terms. He gave up all concern for his forearm that remained in her clutches.

"Well done, Yeshua!" the sage exclaimed. "Amen. A man must take care of his wife: 'he is not to diminish her food, her clothing, or her marriage rights.' But isn't the wife capable of tearing down that which the man builds up? Otherwise, how is it that she is called his 'equal-in-power' at the Dawn of Creation?"

Yeshua responded, "Didn't the man and woman do violence to the designs of HaShem? Therefore, He pronounced during their expulsion from the Garden, 'Your desire will be toward your husband, and he will rule over you.'"

Yeshua's voice sounded far away for the moment. Yosef was becoming lost in thought again. For all the excitement, he found himself surveying the whole of his marriage, wondering if he was living up to his own son's standards of a husband's care and kindness. Whether his arm had gone numb or Miriam had finally relaxed, he couldn't tell.

He loved Miriam beyond compare. His only regret in life was in not providing more comfort and wealth for his family, try as he might. His conscience was clean regarding his conduct. In true humility, he was an ideal husband and father, as strong as he was patient, kind as he was clever. Even so, he knew that he must ask Miriam a litany of questions once they returned home. Listening to his son, he couldn't help but wonder if he should have built his wife up better somehow. Perhaps they would share a pomegranate on the terrace-roof of their house after they prayed Havdalah over Shabbat. Whatever might come in conversation, he wanted to watch the sun and moon in their passing in the company of his wife.

"Are you saying, Yeshua, that a man has power to rule over his wife inasmuch as Cain was supposed to master the sin that was lurking at his door?" the teacher rejoined. "Can a husband control his woman so?"

"Does a man control his own garden, Rabbi? Or does he rather cultivate it lovingly?" Yeshua responded. "How much less should a man presume to master his bride whom he should rather love as his very sister?"

"All right, Yeshua. If HaShem, blessed is He, spurns divorce as much as you imply, then why would He make provisions for it? Does He not prohibit those things He finds detestable, those offenses He considers an abomination?" Nechemyah was calling Yeshua to a final account.

And then Yosef became fully present to the moment. He realized that Yeshua was not sitting next to him any longer, that his son had not been sitting there for longer than Yosef had any way of recalling. At some point, Yeshua installed himself at the head of the synagogue with the sage, seated beside him. Their exchange had become front and center.

It was not like Yosef to panic. However, a wooden dread tangled in his guts like a knotty wane in a stubborn timber. Yosef began stroking his beard in his stress. His right hand found the small bare patch of skin beneath the left side of his jaw. No one could ever see it, but that spot always bothered him, until moments like these when it became something of a talisman in his flesh.

As he surveyed the room, all he could see was a gathering of people who remained transfixed by the exchange before them. If anyone had taken offense at the impropriety, they were not showing it. Nevertheless, he anticipated the relational difficulties that would ensue thereafter. Not for the last time, he found himself bracing for a tenuous middle ground when it came time to discuss the event with

Miriam. By the Throne, this child was a handful.

"Rabbi, did HaShem, blessed is He, wish for manslaughter to occur when He established the Cities of Refuge as a protection for those who have accidentally slain one of their brethren?" Yeshua asked.

Then Yeshua waited.

Nechemyah was stumped. In plain view of all who watched, he was dumbfounded. While his mind raced desperately for a text to draw upon in response, his face went slack.

Yeshua continued to wait.

In the weeks that followed, there would be some dispute as to whether or not Yeshua spoke too soon, whether he had allowed their teacher time to respond or not. Some would say he responded hastily in his presumptuousness. Others would say he was entirely in bounds of propriety, only seizing an opportune moment. Nothing like a consensus on the matter ever developed.

But Yosef was there, painfully aware of the duration of time that passed between the sage's penultimate question and Yeshua's final response. It was an act of compassion when Yeshua would speak again. Indeed, Nechemyah had become naked in his speechlessness.

In that moment, Yeshua acted with more than mercy. He did one of the boldest things Yosef would ever see him do. He assumed the authority to unroll the scroll before the gathering. He revealed a wonder from the Torah. And he did it all as the teacher continued to stand by, adrift in his helplessness.

Yeshua turned his posture from the sage and faced the assembly.

"In the truest of truth, I say unto you that the provision for divorce is tantamount to the Cities of Refuge. HaShem, blessed is He, knowing the hearts of men, has allowed for divorce even as His Soul detests it. He would see men and women sundered from one another before He would see the wickedness of murder become the rule in marriage. However, His heart has always been, and will remain, for the endurance of His creation. And the new creature that is a man-joined-to-his-wife is the Climax of all Creation, even to this very day that remains true before the Maker.

"Woe be unto us if the prophet's words would ever accuse anyone sitting here today:

> 'You cover the altar of Adonai with tears, with weeping and sighing, because He does not regard the offering anymore, neither receives it with goodwill at your hand. Yet you say, "Why?" Because Adonai has been witness between you and the wife of your youth, against whom you have dealt treacherously, though she is your companion, and the wife of your covenant. But did He not make you one, although He had the remnant of the Ruach? Why one? He seeks godly offspring! Therefore, take heed to your spirit, and let no one deal treacherously against the wife of his youth. "One who hates and divorces," says Adonai, God of Yisrael, "covers his garment with violence!"'"

Then, Yeshua left the front of the synagogue and returned to his seat next to Yosef, as unassuming as if he had simply slipped in a little tardy for the gathering.

Everyone sat in a pensive, reverent silence, Miriam and Yosef equally so. Several minutes passed before anyone so much as stirred in their seats. It would be the longest unintended stretch of a peopled quiet that synagogue would contain in all its years.

Eventually, Nechemyah collected himself enough to conclude their time together. All in attendance recited the final prayers. The significance of the event they had witnessed quelled with a profundity that hovered like dense clouds over the countenance of all gathered.

Before leaving, Yosef made it a point to bolt straightway to their teacher. The carpenter's body language expressed deference and respect. His words conveyed gratitude for Nechemyah's service. He had hoped many would notice. Above all, the father of the messiah meant to protect and insure the dignity of their teacher. He anticipated weeks of such exchanges in making amends.

As Yosef returned to his family, preparing to leave, he felt something from across the way. When he turned, he found that it was their centurion benefactor who had been waiting to be seen. Most of the Gentiles had already removed themselves from the synagogue. There was an implicit understanding amongst all of the Jews that they were indebted to this one particular Roman. Nevertheless, the rules of ritualistic separation were ever before them.

The centurion was smiling wide without bashfulness. Yosef knew the admiration of a father when he saw it. Gaius was congratulating Yosef for the wisdom and stature of his son. For a moment, the cultural inner turmoil within the father of the messiah was at complete rest. In that instant, the multifarious complexities of their warring cultures were on the other side of the world, and they were simply two men sharing a silent understanding in the companionship of men of authority born into difficult times.

The father of the messiah smiled back, unabashed. The compliment was not lost on him. Truly, he was grateful for this enigmatic, utterly human exchange. The two men traded their customary nods. And then the moment was gone.

Everyone exited the synagogue in a spirit of reflection. Parting conversations were sparse. Each family went home with a purpose.

Fathers and mothers in every household put their children to bed early that evening. Thereafter, every husband and wife with a suitable rooftop sat alone together, beneath the heavens. All eyes were on the moon that night. The time between each couple was imbued with laughter, the visiting of memories, the renewal of their own stories.

Yeshua looked after his younger siblings as his parents isolated themselves atop the house. He was a very good big brother. Miriam doted upon Yosef, giving her affectionate touch to one arm in particular with a special tenderness.

Love rekindled oversaw the sharing of many pomegranates beneath the glow of that faithful witness in the sky.

4

A Trade and Torah

THE NEXT MORNING, Yosef stirred from his bed later than usual. Immediately upon waking he prayed, "Blessed is He Who gives sight to the blind." As he sat up out of bed he prayed, "Blessed is He Who sets the captives free." When he dressed himself, he prayed, "Blessed is He Who clothes the naked." And when he put his sandals on, he prayed, "Blessed is He Who provides for all my needs." Yosef then donned his tefillin and tallit and recited the Shema.

Miriam was still sound asleep. Yosef smiled to himself, enjoyed the sight of her at rest. Her repose was his delight. The only experience to match it was that of watching his children asleep at night, safe and secure from the worries of the world.

As he left their bedroom and went into the common area of their little abode, Yosef found Yeshua already fully awake and alive to the day. As was his habit, the future messiah occupied his favorite corner of the room, consumed in Torah study, his tefillin drawn up over his head, nearly covering his eyes. He swayed a little, presenting his entire body to the work, as he recited quietly within the hush of the dawn.

Yosef's family kept many secrets. That Yeshua would become the messiah was foremost of them all. Another tacit discretion was the Torah scroll that Yeshua himself had transcribed. Only family knew about it, and only the closest family at that.

Were anyone else to find out that there was a complete Torah scroll in their household, friends and neighbors would begin all kinds of rumors on the matter. The only rational conclusion would be that someone had stolen it. Yosef had never acquired the kind of wealth to possess a Torah scroll.

No, Yeshua had copied the entirety of it himself, according to all of the traditions and halakhah of the scribes. And it was beyond bizarre that he would do so. It was an inconceivable endeavor, absolutely unimaginable to most adults, let alone a child.

Not only had he done it, but Yeshua had done it scrupulously. His scroll was accurate to every letter and refined to every flourish. Were it known to the purveyors of such things, it would have sold for no less than two years' worth of wages. Yosef had to admit that the thought had occurred to him during a few of their more desperate seasons. But when it really came down to the warp and woof of the problem, whatever that might be at the time, he could never do that to his son. It took Yeshua seven years of spare time and scrap parchments to complete his Sacred Text.

The Torah of the messiah was beautiful.

Yeshua was only five years old when he began the undertaking. At first, his tutor thought that it was a curious matter to see a fledgling Torah initiate copying the text during his studies. However, once he realized that Yeshua had taken his writ all the way to Noach and the Flood in his duplication, he took the issue up with Yosef directly. After all, it could not go without vetting where exactly Yeshua was getting his materials.

When Yosef confronted Yeshua about the issue, the child responded with that humble audacity of his.

"If all the kings of Yisrael were commanded to copy the Torah, then how much moreso the messiah?"

Yosef blanched and reddened all at once when he heard those words. Straightway he went to Miriam in a fluster.

"How dare you tell our son that he is the messiah? He has not even become a son of the commandments yet! Already, you would burden him with his future?" Yosef raged.

Miriam responded with equal force and anger.

"I have told him no such thing, Yosef! How is it that you would come into my kitchen with accusations without question? What is this nonsense that you bring in here?"

As Yosef proceeded to relay the events to Miriam, he watched the full heaviness hit her. And then she simply nodded, as she always did when it came to a newfound realization concerning their son. Yosef could never understand how she pivoted in her emotions so nimbly, unencumbered by the weight of bias or preference. But it softened him, regardless.

They were in this together. Just the two of them. He apologized profusely. She forgave him readily.

Yosef and Miriam would discuss many things for several weeks after that conflict, working as well as they could to come to a resolution in their plans for the future. After all, no one had ever raised a messiah before. They were inventing the uniqueness of their diligence as they went.

Most of their curiosities would be postponed for years, even the reverent yearnings. But the angst of wonder over their unusual child never waned. After all, how did their little boy come to know of his destiny at such a tender age?

Those matters would have to wait for some time. Immediately, they had to ascertain for certain that Yeshua had not been stealing his parchments and ink. They were astounded to hear their clever student explain his resourcefulness to them. It would turn out that scribes were especially picky regarding their materials. Yeshua could acquire everything for free with the trick of a little Torah debate and a heap of gratitude. Surely the Scribes had no notion of what this boy was doing with their seconds. Nevertheless, they were endeared to his prodigious interplay in dialogue. And the child knew how to be charming whenever it was expeditious to his purposes. In truth, Yeshua was so savvy with people when he wanted to be, Yosef wondered why the child didn't exercise his charms more often. Isn't that what children with such capacities do?

Yosef felt the shock of time as those memories were simultaneously distant yet right before his eyes. He felt it all over again, groaning a bit within himself, to see that same little five-year-old now a young man before him, fully thirteen years of age, masterful in his trade and sagacious in his studies. For all the painstaking choices Yosef had made over the years, in moments like these it felt as though life rushed over most of him like a raging river while some other part of him was nothing but a helpless witness on the shore, being at once frozen and adrift in his experience of time.

The father of the messiah watched his son study with affection and awe. How many parents would ever witness this indescribable wonder? Yosef mused that it could only ever be two. At the moment, it was only one. The waters of time would sink him eventually, to be sure. Come what may, whether he found himself swimming or treading, he could not help but cherish the currents that would ferry him to such a sight as this: his son, the messiah, and his very own Torah.

Yosef did not hurry Yeshua away from his engagement. He never needed to. His son had long been disciplined with his time. Yeshua was ever diligent, and he respected his apprenticeship as much as he hallowed his Torah studies.

After they had both eaten and concluded their morning prayers, Yosef and Yeshua entered the workshop adjacent to the house. Their donkey, Shimshon, continued to munch away at his breakfast. Yeshua had fed the beast before he began his studies, and the animal was notorious for laboring at his meals with more time and attention than his labors.

Wordlessly they began their activities. Each carpenter knew his place at their respective timbers. Rarely did they work on the same piece of wood at the same time. There was so much knocking, scraping, paring, drilling and chiseling in carpentry that it would have been impossible for two woodworkers to engage the same object without messing up each other's tasks.

The day's work was already before them. Save for a few passing requests of "Hand me that paring chisel, please," or "Could you help me nudge this trestle?" they did not speak at all for the first couple of hours. This was their normal manner together. Never having discussed the matter directly, they simply understood how to work in unison without introducing noise into the morning too early. They liked each other's company, very much so. It just so happened that they liked it in quiet, too.

That being the case, both of them cherished music as well. Yosef was prone to whistle, and his range was rather impressive. Yeshua preferred to hum, and his melodies were lovely.

Often Miriam would serve lunch to them in the workshop, especially when they were too dug into their work to pay any attention to the hours. She delighted whenever she found them each in their own space of song, one whistling, the other humming, neither one of them realizing that they had slipped into a harmonious lilt together. It was another one of countless things she treasured all to herself. As much as she would have loved to tell them about it, she never wanted to run the risk of ruining it.

After a few hours of working in their characteristic quiet, Yosef took the initiative of conversation. He took no pleasure in the thought of where this discussion must go, but he couldn't shake the burden of a father's responsibility. As marvelously as Yeshua had composed himself at synagogue the day before, he knew he had to speak to his son about the impropriety of the matter. Then to address his kingship.

Before he began the talk, though, Yosef asked for Yeshua's help with a shared task. He wanted to test the joinery between two timbers. This feat was nearly impossible alone.

Father and son set the timbers, aligning everything with exact-
ing precision. With mallets and buffer-blocks they began hammering
them together, knocking in time, in a rhythm that they established
between themselves years ago.

But in the last year, they had been able to draw upon a new trick
in the operation. Everyone laughed at Yosef once he hatched the idea
to train the donkey for carpentry, but he was determined in spite of
the jeers. Dissenters were often motivators.

After the timber joint had been aligned, before it was completely
set, they called Shimshon, the donkey, into place. Yeshua braced the
joinery opposite his father; Yosef stood on the other side with Shimmy.
What would happen next everyone had to see to believe. And no matter
how many times they saw it, they never ceased laughing about it.

The master carpenter took hold of a long, thick paddle that he had
hewn for just this purpose. The handle was so long that it allowed him
to stand the length of a man's height away from the point of the strike.
He had attached a supplemental handle that shot off at a sharp angle,
which enabled Yosef to hold the contraption upon his hip and apply
leverage against the downward drag of the weight.

Shimmy's hindquarters were pointed toward the timber joint.
Yosef held the thick end of the paddle over the joinery. At the sound of
two quick bursts of a single note from Yosef's sharp whistle, Shimmy
kicked backwards with a solid leg. And the timber joint compressed.

They repeated this maneuver a few times before the distance
between the joinery was nearly invisible. Each time, Yeshua braced,
Yosef whistled, and the donkey kicked.

Before the final stroke, Yosef nodded to Yeshua, at which point his
son doubled down into his stance. Yosef gripped the paddle firmly once
more. Then he whistled one long, shrill note that fell off all of a sudden.

At the plummet of that note, Shimmy kicked backwards with
both rear legs. It was enough to knock a full-grown man into last
week, perhaps enough to kill him. In this case, it set the joint to perfect

compression. For the absurdity of the sight, its efficiency could not be disregarded.

Father and son cheered and patted Shimmy with enthusiasm. He always earned a treat to munch on for his labors. They could never toil him overlong, but they could always rely upon his kicks so long as they didn't overdo it. The beast saved them from many hours of blisters.

The father of the messiah was proud of himself for his training. Other carpenters, better off, often had fancy machines that had been engineered with counterweights, pulleys and levers. Yosef did not have the space to erect something similar for himself. But it didn't matter. None of the other carpenters could lay claim to his inimitable whistle or his peculiar donkey.

Yosef positioned himself right next to Yeshua as they sat down to rest for a moment. Unless they were in a hurry, their habit was to take a break for water after a successful joint had been paired. The rhythm of the workshop was its own delight.

"You did very well for yourself yesterday with the teacher, Yeshua!" Yosef complimented. And he meant it.

"Thank you, Abba!" Yeshua beamed with delight. The messiah yearned for his father's approval no less than other boys. "To be honest, I was wondering what you thought about the whole exchange."

"Oh... it was rather exciting, most certainly," Yosef assented. "I'm sure the entire community will be discussing it for several weeks."

"Do you think that I upset anybody in the synagogue?" Yeshua asked.

"Probably, my son," Yosef conceded. "But they will be fine. The Torah is meant to scrape at our bark every once in a while. You gave the people nothing short of the Truth. How they square with it afterward has to do with them, not you."

"Hmm." Yeshua ruminated.

Yosef was accustomed to that note from his son. It meant that he was considering innumerable points of reflection, viewing them from his multi-faceted lens of the Torah, letting the Light refract in a thousand different ways, discerning the worth of everything through the font of faithful scrutiny. He might spend the rest of the day in that space. Which was fine with Yosef. Some of his conversations with his son had already spanned years. He did not fool himself to think that certain subjects could do with anything less than several years more.

Yosef might have to interrupt his son's reflections today, however. He had been putting it off for months as it was, and besides, they had the matter of the synagogue to discuss. He intended to bring up the weightier matters last week... and then the horrible crucifixion business came before them in that onslaught of tears.

The father of the messiah was in a predicament the likes of which no other person in the history of the world could possibly relate. At the same time, it was not unlike the struggles that all parents encounter. How much space should he give? How much nearness should he maintain? Was he moving too fast? Too slow? Was his child growing up as he should?

Was Yosef fulfilling his responsibilities? At the end of it all, this kingly carpenter could only act as well as he knew how. Whatever shortcomings might occur in his efforts, he would have to leave those in the hands of the Maker. Didn't He hold even the king's heart like water in His own hands?

Once again, Yosef forced himself to relent. He was not acting alone. The messengers that visited himself and Miriam at the very beginning; the illustrious visitors from afar come to bear witness to the long-awaited messiah; the blessings and prophecies spoken over them during their son's infancy; their deliverance from the murders of madmen; their preservation in the everyday; the whole story of his entire family was ongoing proof that God Most High, blessed is He, walked before them, behind them, beside them, roundabout them.

Yosef chuckled out loud at himself. How much could go wrong, really? The time had come to address the matter of Yeshua's training and preparation as Messiah.

For everything that they had come through, how is it that he found himself so dreadful about a simple talk with his son? Sure, it was heavy, but so was their love. He could not draw out the details of it, but he could engage. A house is framed one timber at a time. The beginning must simply be to begin.

In the very instant that Yosef inhaled to initiate the topic with Yeshua, his son spoke first.

"Do you think Rabbi Nechemyah will be upset with me?" Yeshua asked.

That breath that Yosef had taken in came out as interrupted relief. It was somewhere between a sigh and a heave. He collected himself before he responded, having mustered himself for a different approach.

"Well... I wouldn't worry about that too much, son," Yosef reassured. "The sage is a kindly man. And he is wise. Had you whittled away at him any differently, we would have had a different discussion on the matter. No, I think your relationship will be just fine."

"Are you sure, Abba?" Yeshua pressed.

Yosef could tell that his son heard more behind his thoughts. It was true that he had intended to say more, but in his own time. He just didn't like it when his son knew his thoughts before he spoke them. Nevertheless, not liking it did nothing to change it.

"All right, Yeshua. Shall I speak to you plain, then?" The father sincerely asked permission.

"Always, Abba." Yeshua meant it. There was no pretense between them.

Yosef had no wish to tamp down his son's recent victory. The burden of mere existence upon him was as solitary as it was unique. Shouldn't he be entitled to a few fleeting moments of relief? Regardless, it had come time to score the line.

"My son, it is not your place to install yourself at the seat of authority, teaching as though you had already come into your vigor." Yosef was calm but stern.

"Do you believe that the sage understands the Scriptures better than I do, Abba?" Yeshua asked, earnestly at that.

"Well, my son... that depends on how we consider knowledge," Yosef replied. "Surely, you have greater technical expertise in the matters of mitzvot. I'd also wager that you know the history of our people better than he does, both inside and outside of the Writings. In fact, there may not be a single matter of Torah in which Nechemyah would outclass you... save one."

"What is that?" Yeshua's face lit up as he wondered.

It was one of his most endearing qualities. To be confronted with something that he did not know was never threatening to Yeshua. He relished the opportunity to learn evermore.

"Life," Yosef said flatly.

"Life... Abba..?" Yeshua was quizzical.

"That's right, son. The sage has lived a full life. Whatever he teaches is supported by wizened years and a community that knows his deeds. They know that they can trust him because they have witnessed his years." Yosef could tell that this distinction was not sifting well with his son yet.

"He could still be an Elder in the community if I were teaching, right?" Yeshua returned. "I don't understand why an inferior understanding of the Torah should be at the head of the synagogue."

"Oh boy... take care that you don't say something like that to anyone else..." Yosef whistled.

"I know that, Abba," Yeshua said, a little crestfallen.

"Of course, Yeshua. I'm sorry. You are always respectful. I just worry sometimes, for your sake," Yosef conciliated.

"I know, Abba," Yeshua reassured.

The brief hurt was passed. Father and son carried on as if it had never happened, fully restored to each other.

Yosef reached for the slender shaft of an arrow, a remnant from a previous order. He held it aloft as he portrayed the lesson to his son.

"Look at it this way, Yeshua. Your life is like an arrow. So is mine. So is Nechemyah's. Everyone's life has a beginning and an end. And I don't simply mean birth and death. Rather, I am referring to the development of your person and the purpose of your days.

During the little years, father and mother fashion the arrow for their child the best they can. We whittle, we sharpen, and we conceal. We keep you tucked away until it is your time.

Once you became a son of the commandments, you began selecting the materials of your bow for yourself. These coming years represent the bending of your bow, of your taking aim for yourself down the path of your intentions in this life.

Your arrow will not begin to leave the bow until you begin to leave our household. Even then, it will be some years before its path is made clear, how true it is to its mark, what its mark even is."

Yeshua continued to look to his father with keen interest, fully engaged. Yosef wasn't exactly telling his son things that he didn't know. However, he was saying it better than his son understood. Knowledge was one thing; wisdom was quite another. That was the worthier part that Yosef meant to impress on his son. It was never enough to simply know something without the expertise to demonstrate it. And that always took time.

"You see... Nechemyah's arrow landed a long, long time ago."

Yosef slapped Yeshua on the back as he joked. They both laughed a little.

"No one is curious about how his life might end up!" Yosef continued. They chuckled again. "With you, Yeshua, it is very different. Truly, you are an expert in the Torah. As we saw last year in the Temple, there may not be a Sage in all Yerushalayim that could contend with your mastery of the texts. Of course, that wasn't exactly the first thing that we learned from the debacle, was it now?!"

At that, Yosef shouldered Yeshua in fun and knocked him off balance just enough to be playful. He was careful to make sure that none of the sharp tools were in their grasps when he did so.

Yeshua groaned and rolled his eyes. "Ab-ba!" But he grinned a little bit, too, despite himself.

"What I mean to say is this. No one can be sure how you will live until you have lived it out a while longer. I have faith in you, my son. I believe that you are becoming a good man, living and training already as to become the best of us. But no one else in the synagogue has any reason for that confidence yet. In truth, it is impossible for them to see you that way. It is no fault of your own, but you are simply too young to have that manner of teaching authority over the lives of your elders with decades beyond you."

Yosef watched as the young messiah considered his father's words carefully. He knew that however Yeshua responded, it would be as sincere as it was incisive. But he didn't know how much longer he could keep up with his son's mind, not to mention his ambitions. If the noble carpenter had not reached his son with the imagery of a bow and arrow, he did not know what else he might appeal to in order to instruct him any further.

"Then how will I know when I am ready, Abba, when it's appropriate?" Yeshua asked with conviction.

The father of the messiah spoke with equal measures of authority and gentleness. "When you are invited, Yeshua."

Yeshua looked into his face with a spirit full of power. It wasn't impertinent but it was precocious, not rebellious but challenging. Of all people, Yeshua could only look at his father this way, with his emotions unveiled. Very few adults could have withstood his gaze, with an intensity he kept hidden from others. Even fewer would have seen it as anything other than indignance.

However, Yosef understood him. He knew there was not an insolent bone in his son's body. But the young messiah was a great soul.

Rarely could Yeshua be fully himself, heedless to the needs and perceptions of others. His father was one of a few men in the entire world constituted to be in the company of his son as he was within himself. It was an ongoing gift that Yeshua very much needed in his basic humanity and continual growth. Yosef meant to keep giving it.

What's more, Yosef understood himself. He knew that his son was greater than he was. Heaven's rain – he should hope so if he would amount to anything of a king! As Yosef saw things, it was a tragedy in itself that they did not have a communal infrastructure involved in his training and upbringing. Nevertheless, he still had to raise his son today, whatever the messiah's governance might be tomorrow.

Yosef returned his son's gaze with his own demonstration of power. He was a stalwart soul, too. He simply wasn't the messiah.

They looked into each other's faces with strength, vulnerability and intimacy. Were anyone to walk in upon the moment, they might find themselves wondering whether a fistfight or an embrace would ensue. To father and son, however, they were merely present to each other. They beheld one another as men do, in the enclave of those they trust and esteem.

Their friendship was ferocious. For all the challenges of such a prophetic charge, Yosef cherished the privilege to be a father to a son so magnificent as this, messiah or no. Yeshua was a gift; Yosef was ever delighted to receive him.

After what seemed like an age, Yeshua nodded his head in submission. Then he turned his eyes from his father and went back to his work. And that was the end of the matter.

Yosef waited a moment to ensure that the conversation was over. Once again, he watched his plans disintegrate before him. They had said nothing about the urgency of his kingship. But what they had said was sufficiently demanding. The father of the messiah deemed it best not to lay too many burdens at one time upon his son's shoulders. A single chisel could only pare so much before it required sharpening. Yosef saw the spaces between these talks with Yeshua in the same grain.

After a few moments had passed, Yosef resumed chiseling an inlay of filigree into the entry arch of Sh_omo's pergola. Yeshua remained at the brace that he had been working on and pared away at the curvature. Their companionable silence enveloped them in their labors together.

Before too long, Yosef picked up another tune in his whistle. Yeshua hummed to himself. They harmonized more often than not. Neither one of them ever knew it.

5

Down by the River

ZECHARIYA, ELISHEVA AND their son, Yochanan, were visiting the family. Yochanan was 6 months older than Yeshua, but whenever they were together, nothing separated them. Yosef never saw Yeshua as free in his boyishness as when his favorite cousin was around. The good father delighted to see his son come so alive.

Yochanan was portly, rowdy and set apart. His face hadn't yet grown into the plumpness of his cheeks, which preserved a boyish charm despite his ruddiness. The Essenes with whom they lived had withdrawn themselves from all Roman impositions and Grecian luxuries; their lives were accordingly austere and rigorous. Therefore, the lad was undeniably strong. His hair, curly as it was, had grown all the way down below his waist, making for locks that were lusciously thick. On that day he had pulled his hair back and tied several strands of twine around the tail. Even drawn and bound, it was statuesque just how dense his hair was in accentuation to its length. Women envied his mane, uncovered as it always was. Most importantly, his hair was a constant reminder of the story of his designation as a Nazir since birth.

Yosef suspected that Yochanan was Yeshua's favorite person in the entire world. There was a sense of absolute ease about the young messiah whenever he had his cousin about. Yeshua was almost always relaxed, but he was rarely carefree. He was nothing but uninhibited with his cousin.

Yochanan had a special knack for bringing all of the fun right out of him, out into the world that they would eventually subdue together, or so they schemed. The two of them were inseparable. Yosef had never heard so much as a cross word pass between them. Watching the boys at play, occasionally overhearing snatches of their conspiracies, Yosef wondered if King David and Prince Yochanan of old would have had such a childhood had their years together begun sooner.

On that day, however, something was amiss.

The boys always shared their favorite things with each other. As it was, both of them yearned for waters just as much as the other. Even when these family gatherings occurred during the winter, Yeshua and Yochanan would visit the River whenever possible.

They had all made a day's journey to the River Yarden and camped along its banks the previous night. Needing to return to Natzeret before sunset, they had broken down camp and packed their belongings that morning. The four of them were enjoying their last moments by the waters before their return home.

Yosef relented on his working engagements when family was visiting. He and Zechariya got along almost as famously as the boys did. They didn't talk about their struggles much, not directly anyhow. Nevertheless, they shared in the fellowship of inordinate responsibility, as they were fathers to sons fated for greatness. What passed between them without speech could never be explained to a body that had not been initiated into the bearing of such a burden. They found an unshakable bedrock of friendship in that affinity.

The two fathers watched from the top of an embankment as the boys played down by the River. Yeshua and Yochanan had removed their outer garments and slung them over tree limbs at the banks. More carefully, they had placed their tefillin within a satchel and suspended it from a branch, not wanting to damage the containers or their contents with the waters.

The women had remained at the house with the other children, content to stay indoors and sit together with hot drinks and fresh dates. It was such a delightful arrangement between families that everyone had their winsome counterpart.

Yosef sat down next to Zechariya and then feigned an apology. "I'm so sorry, most holy Essene, sir. Have I sat too close to you? I wouldn't want to corrupt your purity."

"Oh, go wash your hands again, Pharisee!" Zechariya chided.

The men laughed together. Their trust and endearment allowed them to rib at each other's differing practices of halakhah. They were respectful... most of the time.

"How is it, raising him in the wilderness?" Yosef asked. "You Essenes are so withdrawn from everybody. Are you ever concerned that he will be too isolated to understand people?"

"Absolutely, Yosef! Absolutely." Zechariya said. "I fretted over a great many things during Elisheva's pregnancy. Of course, I had to do my worrying away in silence, as you know!"

They both laughed together. Yosef never mentioned those times, unsure of how it would affect his friend. He was always relieved when Zechariya would welcome him into that space of remembrance. Yosef suspected that Zechariya understood the unspoken between them.

The old man was all wrinkles and wiles. He seemed to always be smiling. His eyebrows were so shaggy that he tucked them up into his turban, otherwise they would have obscured his vision. He was a short man, but his presence enveloped everyone. Even in retirement from his Levitical duties, withdrawn into the remote territory of the Essenes, he wore the vestments of the priesthood. The checkered linens flecked with blue and adorned with a purple sash had him ever wrapped in splendor. Zechariya wore the weight of glory well, neither as a boast nor a burden, only embodying the imagery of priestly mediation.

"No, Yosef," Zechariya continued, "I try not to worry too much anymore. I am getting too old to lose any more days to that nonsense. And I do like having my tongue back to myself, believe me, young man!"

Yosef chuckled even though he tried not to.

"Can you imagine a man at my age being struck deaf and mute again, having to scribble away on a piece of slate all the time?" Zechariya chided. "However, as old as Elisheva and I have already become, perhaps our hearing is not so far from lost that we won't be gesturing at each other madly, fussing over our slates together!"

The father of the messiah laughed ruefully and shoved at his friend, but just a little. It was true that Zechariya was aged. And it was also true that he was a worthy man. Yosef would restrain his strength in their playful exchanges, but he would not withhold it altogether. That would have been disgraceful to this noble soul chosen to raise a prophet.

"All right, Zechariya, you old man!" Yosef jested. "Why don't you go ahead and answer my question while I still have you in the land of the hearing! I don't want to leave you here all by yourself while I have to run off and find something for you to scrawl at in your decrepitude."

"Oh, shame Yosef, shame!" Zechariya played the injured party. "And here I thought that we were having a friendly conversation. Now it seems my nephew-in-law is already making plans for my estate..."

"Quite right, most noble elder. Forgiveness, please," Yosef playfully conceded.

They shared nothing but the best of regards for one another.

"You must remember, my friend, that we are not in any way alone with the Essenes," the priest said.

"Oh, right, of course not, Zechariya," said Yosef. "But they are a... peculiar lot... are they not? How is Yochanan to come out of a gathering like that, secluded for years, and bring a message to Yisrael?"

"I will tell you the truth, Yosef,' said Zechariya. They had jested enough to approach the seriousness of the matter. "I learned many things during that time." It took Yosef a moment to realize that the old man was referring to his months of muteness.

"Surely, HaShem, blessed is He, knew what He was doing with me. The only way to endure all of the trials of that time was to trust in

His good providence. He brought me into a very deep and secret place during that silence. After so many months of being mute, the quiet simply sank down into me, down into places that I did not even know were there to be found. It is difficult to explain, but nothing has been the same ever since."

Yosef believed everything Zechariya said, even the parts that went unexplained, especially those parts.

"After dwelling in such a deep, do you hear... anything else..?" Yosef asked, wide-eyed, leaning in, hushed. He was hesitant to even mention too much in his question.

"Ah, Yosef. Always straight to the heart of the matter." Zechariya clasped Yosef's hand for a brief moment. "Do not let this disappoint you, my friend. But you must know. I have heard from neither angel nor HaShem, blessed is He, since I was struck all those years ago."

Yosef reflected on his own encounters with angels, but those were visions within dreams. Zechariya had actually witnessed Gabriel inside the Temple with his very eyes! That level of prophecy was something Yosef could scarcely imagine. And Zechariya was so unpretentious, a stranger would never have reason to suspect such a transformative encounter on his part.

Zechariya looked at Yosef's face for a moment, judging his reaction, which was disappointed, to be sure.

"You must understand, Yosef," Zechariya continued, "that ever since then I have never been let down! Neither have I felt alone. Would that all men come to know such silence! It's true, I have not entertained another visitor. I do not receive words from the heavens." Zechariya closed his eyes for a moment and breathed deeply. "But I hear His song everywhere."

Yosef looked at his friend in a mixture of wonder and confusion. Zechariya was born to the Tribe of Levi, raised in the rhythms and duties of a priest, trained and studious in matters of Torah. And then there was his son, Yochanan. The lad was as untamed as a Golden Jackal, heedless to the concerns of polite society. But he was good, growing up straight and true, which could only be on account of Zechariya's and Elisheva's upbringing, isolated in the wilderness as they were. That they could properly discipline such a rambunctious youth, aged and bending as they were, that was no small thing to esteem.

In the close companionship of his friend, Yosef felt like he was sitting next to himself. What's more, the priest's counsel was inestimable in its wisdom and kindness. The father of the messiah placed more trust in Zechariya than in his own thoughts. So it was that the priest had the carpenter's attention. Yosef did not understand what this "song" was or the urgency of listening for it. But it was Zechariya who said it. Yosef would relent and submit to this man he esteemed as better than himself.

The old man fell silent for a long while, stared off into the horizon, and then he closed his eyes. Yosef would never admit this passing fear to anyone, but, as a matter of fact, Zechariya became so perfectly still in his silence that the carpenter wondered if his friend had not actually passed on into Gan Eden! It was just the briefest of moments – enough to become a self-deprecating memory – before the old man breathed audibly beneath those harkening skies.

Yosef waited several moments for Zechariya to open his eyes and return to conversation. But he persisted in that space, inhabiting the quiet, listening to... Yosef knew not what. So, after looking down at the boys in play, looking around for happenstance passers-by, looking around for anything to be looked at, Yosef closed his eyes, too.

He was restless for a minute, being unsure of this space, but that passed quickly enough. He found that he was carried along into a strange and familiar comfort quite readily. Even though Yosef was ignorant of where he was going, or how to get there, the presence of this priest that he respected so dearly, inhabiting a secret place with which he was clearly intimate – it soothed Yosef's anxieties and helped him to simply be.

Yosef could never recount how long they sat there like that. He never heard anything, either, not a word from above nor this mysterious "song" Zechariya spoke about. But many things in him settled during that time, or at least began to. And in spite of what he didn't hear for himself, he could tell that this old soul beside him was hearing it. That alone could have sustained him for a decade.

In the meantime, Yosef would hear many things. They were the sorts of things that one hears all the time but doesn't heed, whether for hurry or carelessness. As he listened, his spirit began to settle. It was subtle, but he felt the mundane tension of the day sink down into the ground, taking with it particular worries and putting them to bed, at least for a spell.

The River Yarden was a tame waterway. Yosef listened to the murmuring rocks in the soft river rapids. At first it was nothing more than the steady drone of drifting waters. As he listened longer, he could begin to isolate various pockets of miniature waterfalls. In some places it sounded like the river tumbled over itself in a hurry, as if various currents were jostling for an advance position; at others it seemed like little streams would slide across a boulder in an unending game of evasion.

Much further downriver he noticed, for the first time, hippopotami in their rut. Crocodiles were fighting each other over a recent kill. Loons played their own games in the water, unconcerned with the boys in their proximity. Overhead the albatrosses glided atop the breeze, taking no path but that of soaring in place. Hoopoes pecked and nestled in the junipers all about him.

Then, immersed in the sounds of Creation, he heard himself. His breathing became simultaneously more conscious as well as more effortless. And without even meaning to, Yosef heard his own heartbeat.

At some point, the two men shook themselves out of their reverie. Yosef realized that Zechariya, through arts unknown to himself, had guided them during their time of quiet together. When Yosef looked at his friend next to him, he saw that the priest's eyes glistened with a sturdy joy. He was not crying, but there was a sure mark of something else that welled up from the deep within him. Zechariya seemed unconcerned at being studied so. He simply smiled at Yosef and clasped their hands together once more.

Zechariya might have spoken of things too mystical for most, but Yosef never knew a man more sound. His head had not gotten so far into the heavens that he was not sure-footed upon the ground. It seemed like the priest had learned how to inhabit both realms.

"Give it a little time each day, Yosef, and you will hear it, too," Zechariya assured. "If you set out to capture it, like a hunter with his traps, it will elude you for the rest of your days. However, if you would wait for it to find you hiding in the stillness, as though a doe might come about you unawares, fast asleep, heedless of the hunt, then you will find yourself all of a sudden pounced upon! And once the heavens have you, you will not be easily removed from their embrace. Neither will you want to be removed. Ah, Yosef! To hear the songbirds in their melodies, the starry hosts in harmony! If I had the skill, I would sing it for you even now. And oh, my friend, when you come to hear the masterpiece of the Maker Himself, may His Name be praised..."

Yosef thought that Zechariya was collecting his thoughts, but he fell silent again for so long that Yosef couldn't take it anymore.

"Well!" Yosef demanded. "What happens then?" It was quite unlike him to be so insistent. It was also highly irregular to have the whole universe suspended before him.

Zechariya didn't flinch in the slightest. He didn't hurry his response, either. He took his time, once again, before answering the younger man in his impetuousness.

The old priest clasped the carpenter's hands within his own. Zechariya gazed deep into Yosef's countenance. Then he smiled that knowing grin that only the wizened and truly wise have earned the right to bestow on others.

"Nothing happens, Yosef," Zechariya said. "Nothing at all happens. Then you find that everything has already happened."

Zechariya released Yosef's hands gently from his grasp. With an understanding nod at Yosef's perplexity, the old man turned his gaze back to the riverbanks where the boys had remained. Yosef followed the old man's eyes, unsure of what to do next. He did not understand. He could not even pretend to begin to understand. But he would wait, like his friend had just instructed him. This was Zechariya speaking, after all.

And then the fight broke out.

All that Yosef and Zechariya could perceive was the clamor of boys at odds. They could not make out any of the words being shouted. Yochanan was shoving Yeshua, like a lad does when he's looking for a good scrap. Yeshua wasn't shoving back, but he wasn't giving his ground away, either. That only served to get Yochanan even more riled up.

Yosef glanced at Zechariya, ascertaining his response to the scuffle. It seemed that both men understood that they should let this play itself out between the boys. This was not like them at all. And the two men were not so far removed from their childhoods as to have forgotten the good that these reckonings often work between the aggrieved parties.

Yochanan had redoubled his efforts to knock Yeshua off balance. Perhaps he only wanted to shove him to the ground to assert his dominance, but that wasn't working out. Yeshua was quite sure-footed. To Yosef, it looked like Yeshua had some trick of shifting his weight imperceptibly, nullifying these jolts from Yochanan.

So, when Yochanan lunged into his final barge and shoved full-force into Yeshua, the young messiah dodged quickly to the side, grabbed Yochanan's nearest arm with both hands, stuck one leg out in front of Yochanan's knees, pivoted, and then heaved Yochanan with all his strength, hurling him face first into the ground. Yochanan skidded a couple of body lengths across the stony riverbank; the skin of his face became a map of that pathway.

Yosef remembered seeing the Romans perform maneuvers like that in the palaestras of their gymnasiums. It never occurred to him that Yeshua might have observed those movements. He wondered how his boy had ever learned the technique well enough to perform it under pressure.

In any event, Yochanan was not the sort of boy to take kindly to being disgraced face first in the dirt.

"Enough, Yani!" Yeshua called out. Yosef made out that much of their exchange very clearly.

Heedless and irate, Yochanan immediately sprang up from the ground and dashed at Yeshua. From the embankment, Yosef could see that Yochanan was winding up to strike Yeshua in the face. As he looked at Yeshua, it did not seem like he was in any way aware that a punch was coming upon him with terrible speed. Yosef winced as he prepared for the impact. His boy was about to find himself on the wrong side of his first knockout. When he stole a glance at Zechariya once more, the old man had his fists clenched. He had a son in the foray, too, after all. Even old priests, it seemed, had a pulse that quickened at the nearness of battle. For a brief moment Yosef remembered the violence of the priest's ancient ancestor, Levi.

Yosef might have been more amused by the display had it not been a family matter.

Everything happened in the most furious and blurring of instants. Just before Yochanan landed his blow, Yeshua tucked his whole body and leaned forward, taking the punch squarely to the top of his head. Yochanan howled like those jackals in the hills when his strike landed on solid bone. Yeshua did not let that note resound before he ducked down, grabbed Yochanan by the hips, and sprang straight back up beneath his cousin's face, driving from the legs, knocking his head backwards as Yeshua's skull collided with Yochanan's chin. That upheaval turned into another sudden delivery to the ground, this time with Yeshua landing right on top of the older, bigger boy.

The plummet was so shattering and unpredictable that both of the older men at last flinched and shouted out.

"Ho!" "Boys!" "That's enough!" "Stop it!" "Right now!"

It didn't matter which man shouted what. Just as they had shared an understanding to let the boys settle this themselves, they were suddenly resolved together to put an end to the matter as the elder adults instead. Yosef wondered if this would not develop into a family dispute, but that would have to wait.

However, before Yosef and Zechariya could scurry down to the riverbank, Yeshua had already ended things on his own terms. Once he had landed on top of Yochanan, Yeshua grabbed both of his cousin's arms and threw them up behind Yochanan's head. He then slid his shin across Yochanan's neck and bore down with all of his weight, still pinning his arms.

Yosef was still running as this all happened, leaving Zechariya a bit behind. He could see that Yochanan would not surrender, too proud and too humiliated to give up yet. Then suddenly, the fight left the older boy entirely. He was subdued.

Yeshua was already standing and offering to help his cousin up by the time the fathers reached the bank. Zechariya picked his boy off the ground, moving past Yeshua's outstretched hand. Yosef took Yeshua beneath his arm and began the journey home, loading their gear upon Shimshon. Each father collected his son's respective clothing and tefillin.

They were several paces away before Zechariya and Yochanan moved along and fell in behind them from a distance. As Yosef looked over his shoulder at the two of them, Yochanan was disconsolate, tucking his right hand beneath his left arm, wincing. Zechariya ever so slightly raised his hand in Yosef's direction, granting a mannish nod, a gesture that communicated that all was well and that everything would be fine. It was enough to reassure Yosef that there would be no impending family feud about the uproar.

As the boys grew older and continued to enjoy their years together, they came to refer to that part of the riverbank as the Yani-brook. Only the fathers ever understood the secret jest. As far as Yosef knew, the boys never found any need to revisit those hostilities as they grew up. They only laughed about it, along with everything else they carried on about.

Confident that they were beyond earshot, Yosef asked Yeshua what in the fool's folly just happened.

"So... how did all that come about?" Yosef raised one assertive eyebrow.

"Well," Yeshua said, rubbing at the top of his head a little, "Yani and I were talking about the Kingdom, like we usually do. Then he said how fun it would be, when we came into the fullness of age, that he would be like Isaiah and I would be like Micah. I didn't mind that comparison so much, but it seemed like the time had come that he should know how it would really be..."

"Oh boy..." Yosef sighed.

"I tried to be gentle about it, Abba," Yeshua insisted.

"I'm sure you did, Yeshua," Yosef reassured. "What did you say?"

"I said, 'Yani, I think that you will become even greater than the prophet Isaiah, but you must understand: I will be more like Hezekiah than Micah, and you will become my first emissary.'"

Yosef whistled.

"You saw the whole thing, Abba?" Yeshua asked.

"We did," Yosef assented.

"So, as you could see, he didn't like hearing that," Yeshua sighed that time.

Yosef let those words hang in the air between them for a few moments. He glanced back at the other two again, finding them in the same condition, Zechariya casting the same reassuring gesture once more. The families would be just fine, even though Yosef hated to think of their wives' reactions.

"Honestly, my son," Yosef resumed, "I was surprised to see the... excitement ended so quickly. It does not seem like Yani to lose his fire that suddenly. May I ask how you finished it?"

Yeshua took a long time to answer that question from his father. Yosef had grown accustomed to these delays in their chats. They could happen at any time, over any subject. It never communicated disrespect on Yeshua's part. Rather, what he would bring himself to say he would then stand by for the rest of his days. Yosef had learned to wait patiently for the words that would endure.

"I did not want to hurt him, Abba," Yeshua said at last.

"I know that, Yeshua," Yosef said. "Believe me, I know how much you love him."

"Even so," Yeshua continued, "I knew that we could not have that contention remain between us, nor any ambiguity. This had to become the first and last fight that would ever pass between us. The last thing that I want is to squelch that holy fire that burns so bright within him. But he could never be allowed to let that flame rise up against me – ever again."

"So, what did you do!" Yosef demanded.

Then Yeshua stopped in his tracks and grabbed his father by the cloak. It was an unnerving display of emotion. Yosef half-wondered, for just a moment, whether Yeshua did not have designs on striking him all of a sudden.

Yeshua looked his father full in the face.

"I asked him if he was prepared to contend with the Almighty."

Yosef remained in his son's grasp for another moment before he was released. They continued walking. The father of the messiah felt no more compulsion for clarity. He kissed his boy gently on the part of his head where he imagined the blows had landed. Then, catching glimpses of his face, Yosef realized that there must have been more fight that he had not witnessed, seeing scrapes and cuts that he could not explain. Yeshua leaned into his father and remained there for a while.

He planned on clearing the air with Zechariya once they arrived at home. Then he began planning out what to say to Miriam... how to say it to her... if he would say it to her...

The four of them finished their hike home in silence, each son in his father's embrace for the first leg of the return. It was a long trek back to Natzeret, several hours at a brisk pace. Their entire day had been devoted to the excursion.

As they approached the ragged outskirts of Natzeret, Yosef reflected on two things, realizations that would occupy his thoughts for much time. The first was that Zechariya never answered his question about raising a child-prophet in the wilderness. His only response was that Prayer of Quiet.

The second was much more disconcerting. He never breathed a word of it to anyone, not even Miriam. When Yeshua recounted his skirmish-ending words to his father, Yosef's entire body trembled, as if deep winter had blown its way into his bones and left the door of his spirit wide open to the winds. Yosef could not recall another instance in all of Yeshua's life in which he sounded so grim and foreboding. Indeed, the father of the messiah was troubled in his reflections.

What in the Valley of Death did Yeshua mean about contending with the Almighty?

6

Sabbath Evening

BY THE TIME the men had arrived back home, the sun was nearly at the horizon and the wives were busy setting the house and the table in order. Everyone had enough time to prepare themselves for the approach of Shabbat, but just barely. This was the normal way of things. No matter how bustling the day had been in its activity, there always seemed to be a single missing hour in preparation for the ceasing to which they would soon enter into and submit. The scurry would continue until the hush right before the lighting of the lamps.

As Yosef collected himself, he more than half-hoped that Miriam would be too preoccupied to notice the cuts, scrapes and bruises that would soon cross over their threshold. If they could only sneak off quietly for the briefest time, the household would soon be under the cover of darkness, dimly lit by the lamplight of Shabbat. Yosef had to be cunning as a snake and sweet as a dove in order to pull this off. There would be no escaping the truth altogether, that much was clear. But if he could only put it off until the morning, once everyone was more composed and well at rest.

Alas. This was Miriam. She was a lioness. Yosef's wife could smell blood.

They all touched the mezuzah at the entrance before stepping into the house. No sooner had Miriam caught sight of them that she whirled her gaze upon Yosef, glanced back at Yeshua, and then locked her demanding eyes on Yosef. As the good carpenter prepared to frame the event in his mouth, Zechariya and Yochanan came in behind him. Yosef was still standing just in front of the door, like a guest who wasn't sure exactly where to move once inside a strange house. Zechariya, on the other hand, was quite comfortable to burst right in, none of the excitement concealed whatsoever, one arm slung across Yochanan's shoulders, his other hand reaching out for Elisheva across the room.

The mother of the prophet, upon seeing her wounded son and her desperate husband, ran to them both with outstretched arms. She was the living image of tender consolation in motion. All manner of cooing and petting and oh-my-dear-ing spilled over upon her two boys. Yochanan was brooding. Zechariya seemed flustered as if he had been the one in a scuffle.

Elisheva never spoke much. Yosef couldn't determine whether this habit developed in her after her miracle of conception, alongside of Zechariya's strickenness, or whether this had been her way all her life. In either case, she carried a strength in her silence. She was taller than Zechariya, a trait that was accentuated by the graceful dignity with which she stood, and she remained strong in spite of her age through the constant exercise of her domestic duties, even more pronounced in their life with the Essenes. Although her linen garments were plain, her blue head covering fell below her waist as a sash that made her look like a queen. Her entire aura of hospitality and nurture was disrupted only by the penetrating gaze of her gray eyes. She seemed to see everything, even those things a person wished to remain concealed... especially those things. Yet the sense of care that she bestowed upon everyone never wavered in the face of that inescapable discernment. Besides, her apple-cheeked smile was even more beautiful in maturity than it had been in her youth. She was a woman of wisdom in every way, the living icon of the daughter of a priest.

As Elisheva continued to ask what had happened, Zechariya

proceeded to shrug, stammer and sigh his way through his non-explanation. Yochanan remained sullen, not looking anyone in the face, not even with his mother's hand beneath his chin, assessing his condition. The gash at the base of the boy's jaw was impressive. Meanwhile, there was no tension between husband and wife as their affectionate hands accosted their unresponsive son.

Yosef marveled at how incompetent Zechariya seemed all of a sudden, and how Elisheva was entirely unperturbed by his behavior. The two of them were strangely bound by an intimacy that remained undeterred in the confusion and scare of it all. It looked as if their togetherness was enough and the details of what exactly had happened would come out in their own time to the vexation of neither husband nor wife.

So, Yosef felt inspired to lean his arm across Yeshua's shoulders and stretch forth his free hand toward Miriam. That inspiration fell away from him as soon as he looked back toward Miriam and saw the furious inquiry of her glare undiminished. This would be no easy night.

Yeshua was doing his very best not to smirk at any of these displays. He almost succeeded. Almost.

With no other notion of what to do in order to start smoothing things over, Yosef spoke across the room to Elisheva who was still comforting both of her boys, one more eagerly in receipt than the other. "The boys had a – misunderstanding – is all, Elisheva. Everything is fine now. They have worked things out." Yosef meant to convey confidence. He knew it didn't work as his tone did nothing to reassure even himself on the matter.

"Why don't you help us – understand – husband?" Miriam demanded.

Yosef wasn't sure why he was in trouble. Miriam looked at him as if he had left the house with her favorite glass only to return hours later with it broken into shards. He had no notion where to begin or how to end once he did begin. This was not the Shabbat that he had been looking for.

As the room looked upon Yosef in his helplessness, Zechariya spoke up.

"Miriam, forgive me, please, I don't mean to interrupt. But I am an old man after all, and Shabbat is coming upon us, and I wonder if I might have your leave to go and make myself ready? At my age, it takes so much longer for me to do even simple things like wash up and change my attire." Zechariya may as well have dressed himself in the regalia of the High Priest with that plea. He would remain unassailable from the impending doom.

Yosef felt like a little boy before a Torah-teacher, caught misbehaving with one of his classmates during class at yeshiva. Only somehow his accomplice had just gotten exonerated and he was holding the bag of trouble all by himself. What had he done wrong? And how could Zechariya just leave him there like that?

The father of the messiah was helpless in his stupor. He watched Zechariya walk away as if from behind the prison gates with the other slaves that had not been emancipated. A free man had been made from the same crime. There would be no justice tonight.

"Yosef, would you mind showing me to your water basin?" Zechariya asked in that same helpless-old-man intonation.

In the instant that Miriam shifted her jaw to the left, Yosef bolted toward Zechariya with all the helpfulness that he could feign. Yeshua would be left to his own devices. It was rare when the good carpenter did not feel the instinct to protect his son. This was one such occasion.

As the two men left the room and proceeded toward the cistern at the rear of the house, Yeshua asked his mother if there was anything he could do to help. Miriam tsked at him to go get ready. Yosef rolled his eyes at how easily everyone else was getting away with things.

As Yosef looked at the wizened fellow beside him, Zechariya grinned at him quietly, and shrugged once more, eyebrows upturned in an expression of "Don't ask me!" If any part of the carpenter had remained skeptical of the secrets to be learned from the prayer of quiet, all remaining doubt fell away as he witnessed Zechariya's effortless escape from the clutches of matrimonial distress. Yosef was still a little sore at the way of things. But he had to admit it. This old priestly uncle of his was a genius.

The skulking carpenter was wary enough to realize that this pretense would only afford him so much time. And he still had things to tend before the sun set upon them. He could trust Yeshua to feed Shimshon. So, he set himself to the stove to dress the fire one last time before they left it alone for the duration of the coming day.

Yosef was quite good with a flame. His intuition prevailed upon many things. Coupled with his understanding of wood and the habits of air, it was a rarity when he could not bend a fire to his will. The trick with the Shabbat flame was to let it burn low, so slowly that glowing coals would remain in the stove until the following evening.

Squatting on his heels and haunches before the stove, he banked the coals toward the back, beneath the egress. Then he loaded the night's worth of fuel upon the embankment, carefully arranging the size and shape of each piece of driftwood so that just enough air would whisper through to keep the coals flickering upon the fuel, but not so much that a heavy blaze would ever be free to erupt.

As he stood up from a well-bedded fire, he felt a presence standing at his back. Instantly, he knew that the real heat was behind him. He turned around to find that Miriam had afforded him only enough room to do just that – stand up and turn around. He was her captive at last.

Miriam gazed at him with the same intensity that he had just narrowly escaped moments ago. Yosef made no attempts at an explanation or a defense. He still wasn't sure what his infraction had been. Indecision left him like a man waiting for his sentencing before the Sanhedrin.

The mother of the messiah, standing tall in her authority as matriarch of the household, grabbed Yosef by the beard in one hand, clutched his cloak at the waist with the other, stood up on her toes, leaned her face resolute into his, and she kissed him at the bare spot of skin right at the corner of his mouth. It was one of her favorite places to kiss him. She lingered as long as it pleased her.

Yosef wasn't sure what would follow, but he would most eagerly accept this as the commencement of his punishment. He remained motionless, unclear as to what allowances he would be permitted with his own face and hands during this exchange. Like the prey in the domain of the lioness, he waited lest he panic.

After moments beyond counting, Miriam released him from her kiss, although she kept him in her clutches. She gazed upon him for another spell, no less intense than the start. Then she waggled his beard with only the slightest tug. At last, she turned on her heels and left him standing there, sheepish.

Miriam was as sultry as she was terrifying. The carpenter had no idea what had just been done to him, even less what had been communicated. But he was surprised, and he liked it. Only once he was sure that Miriam was removed from noticing him did he allow himself a contented little grin. Perhaps the night wouldn't be so bad after all.

And then Zechariya materialized from the shadows at the back of the house. For the way he looked at Yosef, the father of the messiah knew that the priest had witnessed that entire display of his vixen's affections. Yosef was too exasperated to speak in his flummoxed embarrassment, but everything spilled out in his hands and face. Zechariya responded with one hand on Yosef's shoulder, a knowing shrug, and that same whimsical upturn of his greyed and bushy eyebrows, managing to waggle them even though they remained tucked up into his turban. Then Zechariya, too, left Yosef standing there at the stove. The poor man didn't deserve any of this.

Motivated as everyone was not to aggravate hostilities any further, the remaining preparations were finished in short order. The entire family gathered at the table cleaned up, dressed up, and ready to eat. Yeshua's younger siblings had been made ready well before dinner, scurrying about until they had been called to the table. Men returned to the table without their tefillin, having placed them away for Shabbat.

They stood together in a wondrous expectation. In spite of everything, a palpable, visceral peace began to settle upon the house. Everyone knew that their long-awaited and regularly attending guests would soon arrive. Every week it was the same thing. The anticipation never got old.

Elisheva asked Yochanan if he had readied himself for Shabbat.

"I made a mikveh of the River, mother," the stout boy responded, "I am ceremonially clean."

Yochanan wasn't exactly disrespectful at that moment, but he was more than a bit curt.

Elisheva looked to Zechariya with an expression that asked for assistance. Yosef expected him to work his shrug-magic again. Rather, the old priest gave the same raised-hand-nodding gesture that he had given Yosef back at the River. Apparently, Elisheva understood that all was well and that they would sort things out later. The old man was a sorcerer.

With all matters put to rest, Miriam looked to her husband to begin.

Yosef stood at the head of the table, large enough to seat ten comfortably. He was a master carpenter, after all. His usage of space was always clever and innovative and he spared no creativity in his own home whenever he could spare it. The place where they would regularly gather for prayer and dining was sacred to the family rhythms. Its construction portrayed the reverence.

Nearly everywhere in the house were cabinets and cupboards that Yosef had built into the walls, even the ceilings. Blankets, clothes, utensils, parchments, everything had a place. He did not take much time for himself in the way of molding and other such embellishments, but the utility of the household was as efficient as it was becoming.

"Shabbat Shalom!" Yosef called.

"Shabbat Shalom!" everyone replied.

Miriam had a single candlestand in her hand, the candle previously lit from the fire of the stove. She was like a queen in her court as she extended her reach to light another candle on the table. This second candlestand she picked up and handed to Elisheva, which her aunt was ecstatic to receive.

The two matriarchs made a round of the house in a grand, silent ceremony, walking together and taking turns. These were their last minutes to light the various oil lamps they would require for the duration of the night. The men and children held their peace as the women gave their light to the household. When the ladies returned to the table, they set their candlestands at the center. Miriam looked at Yosef in the fulness of adoration, her face aglow in the flames of Shabbat.

The father of the messiah took a moment to look everyone in the face. This was his habit. It had also been an eventful day, especially its closure. He wanted everyone to feel together before they sought the Presence of Another over their gathering. Having shared eyes with each family member in turn, Yosef lifted up his hands, looked to Heaven, and he prayed.

"Blessed is He Who has made us holy through His commandments and commanded us to light the candles of Shabbat."

Yosef always struggled not to let his gaze rest on Miriam during this part of the ceremony. He never tired of looking at her, whatever the time of day. But there was something else about her, every week, in this very hour, before these lights, as if Shabbat was her most native domain and this glow her most natural state.

Everyone gathered at the table saw his hesitation. Their children were accustomed to this break in the sequence, so much so that it had become an integral part of the rhythm. For the other three, however, Zechariya, Elisheva and Yochanan, they were not as accustomed to

Yosef's adorable, unabashed delight in his wife. Of course, they loved seeing husband and wife enamored together. Even Yochanan began to perk up. There was no hurry about anyone that evening.

Nevertheless, the man would have to recollect himself, if only to be a gracious host. Yosef inclined toward Zechariya to trade places with him at the table. After the briefest exchange of refusal and insistence, the priest relented and took the head of the table. The clever carpenter took this as his unusual opportunity to place himself right next to his wife at the table. They held hands together.

The father of the messiah had planned on this gesture of substitution all week, but he did not want to warn Zechariya beforehand, for fear that he would preemptively refuse. Yosef could be conniving when the situation warranted. He had the blood of kings in his keeping, so he could officiate in a grand and elegant manner. But Yosef was not a priest. What Zechariya could perform would be an extraordinary privilege for the entire family. Yosef would not see such an opportunity lost on them.

As if another flame had alighted upon the old man, he seemed suddenly more prominent as he enacted the rites of his training and lineage. It had been over a decade since his service in the Temple had been complete. But all those former years still resided in his frame. The grandeur of his piety made him look taller and his motions grander. Every motion was ornate with subtlety and decorum. Eyes affixed to his officiation in transfixed worship and wonder. The old priest lifted a stone pitcher and a lone glass from the table and poured a serving of wine

"Blessed are You, Adonai, our God, King of the Universe,

Who creates the fruit of the vine!"

Zechariya hesitated at the head of the table. The priest lifted his eyes to Yosef and inclined his head to exchange turns once again. Yosef assented with his body language that it would be appropriate.

Looking over the boys, Yosef blessed them, "May God make you like Ephraim and Manasseh," and over his daughter, Shlomit, "May God make you like Sarah, Rebecca, Rachel, and Leah."

For several minutes, the parents took their time to bless each of their children in turn. They revisited accomplishments and high notes from the week. Both families shared their affections in a dim murmur beneath the lights of Shabbat. Even Yochanan could be seen to drift away from his earlier frustrations and lean into the warm care of his father and mother.

After this unhurried time of peace, Zechariya resumed the prayers at the head of the table. This was the moment Yosef most wanted to receive – the blessing of a priest! The old man lifted both hands in a flourish of authority over everyone, thumbs pressed together at the tips with fingers outstretched in the mirror image of the Hebrew letter shin, signifying the divine presence of the Almighty.

"Adonai bless you and keep you!

Adonai make His face to shine upon you and be gracious to you!

Adonai lift up His countenance upon you and give – you – peace!"

If the lamps had erupted into a firestorm it would have seemed natural. Hands raised high in power, face exalted in blessing, the sun fully set and the stars beginning to break. The warmth of Shabbat had permeated the household. All hearts burst with belonging.

"An accomplished woman who can find?

Her value is far beyond rubies.

Her husband's heart trusts in her, and he lacks nothing valuable."

Just as parents had doted upon their children, husbands and children then praised the mothers. The dinner, the home, their beauty, their virtues – anything and everything came into pronouncement as these creatures of glory beamed in the adoration of their families. Their installation as the aura of light within the household was most conspicuously on display during this exchange of affections every Shabbat. The greater the compliments the children learned to pay to their mothers over the years, the better the husbands liked it.

Zechariya swayed ever so slightly as he proceeded and sang.

"So there was evening and there was morning – the sixth day.
So the heavens and the earth were completed along with their entire array.
God completed – on the seventh day – His work that He made,
and He ceased – on the seventh day – from all His work that He made.
Then God blessed the seventh day and sanctified it,
for on it He ceased from all His work that God intended to create.
Blessed are You, Adonai, our God, King of the Universe,
Who has made us holy through His commandments and has been pleased with us,
and has given us His holy Shabbat as a heritage with love and favor,
as a reminder of the work of Creation in the Beginning.
For that day is the foremost of our holy called-out times,
a remembrance of the Exodus from Egypt.
For You have chosen us and sanctified us from among all the nations.
You have given us Your holy Shabbat in love and delight as our heritage.
Blessed are You, Adonai, who sanctifies the Shabbat."

Yosef possessed a wonderful singing voice, but there were certain qualities that only years could endow. Zechariya had in his keeping all of those years and all of those qualities. A lifetime of priestly training and Temple offerings reverberated in every note of the old man's kiddush. To hear those familiar words and melodies resound, renewed in their antiquity, was an unspeakable privilege.

As the intonations receded in the hush, Zechariya concluded their prayers.

"Blessed are You, Adonai, our God, King of the Universe,
Who brings forth bread from the earth."

Miriam lifted two baskets of challah from the table. It was an offering to God as well as to the families. They all reflected on the double portion of manna before Shabbat in the Wilderness. This moment reminded them of their own double portions on that very day. Everyone was more themselves than any other time of the week. The cessations that defined Shabbat, and everything they would receive in its time, was their good pleasure and delight.

Zechariya lifted up the glass full of wine for all to see and lowered it back down to the table with relentless care. The old man looked to Miriam with a question on his face, then swiftly to Elisheva, indicating his request. Miriam assented her approval that Elisheva should receive the blessing of the cup.

The wizened matriarch cherished the honor. Zechariya brought the cup to her in reverence and affection. After she drank, she immediately delivered it to Miriam, who drank in turn and handed it to her husband. With the exception of Yochanan, everyone at the table enjoyed the blessing of the first cup before they continued in their prayers. The entire family knew to be careful in preserving the sacrosanct designation of Yochanan's vows. However, it was also incumbent on them to enjoy the wine in their delight of Shabbat. The care of one and the pleasure of many shared the same space without conflict.

They all sat upon their cushions and reclined at the table low to the ground. The spread before them was as expansive as it was delectable. Yosef had spared no expense in anticipation of family they loved so dearly and enjoyed so well. The wine they would share this Shabbat was especially delicious. The longer they dined, the louder they laughed.

Such was the way of their Shabbat together. Illuminated by the lamps that irradiated their worship, every faced shone in the gifts and delight of their Maker. In these life-giving, pulsating practices right at the heart of peace and joy, hostilities retreated and merriment ran rampant.

All guests were fully welcome and in attendance. Everyone was home. All was well.

7

Sabbath Morning

EVERYONE SLEPT IN. Everyone. Even Yeshua, who never missed an early morning to study whenever he could help it.

These mornings were most welcome to the parents. Breakfast had already been prepared the day before, so children could help themselves to it whenever they happened to awaken, with no need of Abba or Ima scurrying to satisfy early risers. More often than not, Yosef and Miriam would linger in bed until the pain of hunger overtook the pleasure of rest. Zechariya and Elisheva were more than willing to behave like their hosts, enjoying the other bedroom that had been cleared of children.

Because the weather was fair, the men had erected tents on the flat rooftop for the children the day before. So, the house belonged to the adults for the bulk of the morning, since enterprising parents had the foresight to have the children take their morning's breakfast with them the night before. It was a tiny adventure for the young ones and the exact opposite for the elders. The arrangement satisfied all parties without complaints.

Husband and wife had indeed enjoyed a good night together, and woke up like the married do following such occasions. They delighted in each other's faces in the quiet, unhurried in their repose. Small talk had been inconsequential at first, but it was unavoidable that they returned to unsettled matters at some point. Yosef had been explaining yesterday's scuffle to his wife. Miriam had not yet accepted his response to the matter.

Despite the tension, Yosef was all the more enraptured in the beauty of Miriam on Shabbat. Her hair was uncovered! As long as they remained in their room, her wild, unbound glory was his to behold. The dignity of covering their heads in public was a gift that most of the Jewish wives bestowed upon their husbands; the eroticism of its exposure in private was another gift on the other side of decency.

"Miriam, I must have you know that we didn't just let them fight unchecked. We let it go for a bit, but only to a certain point," Yosef explained.

It was important to both of them not to instigate an argument that would ruin the day. They tried to keep the peace throughout the week, whatever the difficulties, but their commitment to Shabbat elevated this practice to the very forefront of their focus. Rest was their worship on that day and they would protect it together. Nevertheless, the matter was volatile and it wouldn't do well to wait.

"Why would you let them fight at all?" Miriam challenged.

"Come now, my love, you know how boys are. They needed to answer that question at some point. Honestly, I'm surprised that this didn't come between them sooner," Yosef responded.

"No, husband, why would you let *them* fight? You know what they're destined for!" Miriam insisted.

"Miriam, that is all the more reason to give them space to sort it out. And like I told you, it was their eventual relationship that was the heat of their little battle. How do you suspect the two of them would end up if Zechariya and I were always intervening, forcing them to relate to each other according to our demands?" Yosef was calm though resolved.

The mother of the messiah was thoughtful. Her brow was knitted in frustration, but Yosef could tell that she was considering his words. He was wise enough to know that certain things regarding men would always seem ludicrous in the considerations of a woman. Accordingly, he often had to remind himself that the reverse was true whenever he found Miriam's behavior incomprehensible. Men and women were two halves of the same creature, by the designs of HaShem, blessed is He. Nevertheless, the space between them was oftentimes as impassable as the divide between land and sea, as far removed as mountain's peaks and ocean's depths. Although they might share the same air, they would never be the same terrain.

"This far the waves shall come – and no farther!" Yosef murmured to himself.

"What's that?" Miriam asked.

"Oh... nothing... my thoughts just ran to a passage from Job for a moment," Yosef recovered.

"No, Beloved, let me ask you this. What manner of training do you think that I would provide for our son if I were to insinuate myself into his every altercation? Do you think the messiah must learn to do battle at some point? Who is going to lead our armies and fight our enemies?"

"That's ridiculous," Miriam reacted, "that is for a man to do, and Yehoshua is just..."

On Shabbat, she always insisted on saying his full name. It seemed as though something new had occurred to her in saying it again on that day. Yosef looked on as Miriam faltered. He waited and prayed a silent little prayer to HaShem. Perhaps the pieces were clicking together in the reckonings of his wife.

"What is he 'just,' Miriam?" Yosef prodded.

"You know what I want to say, Beloved, but..."

"But he is no longer just a boy, is he, my Lady?"

Miriam remained pensive.

"Dearest, it is natural that you should want to nurture him, to keep him close, as much as it is natural for me to protect him. What you must remember is that since he has come of age, he has left your care and entered into my stewardship. Now, the greater part of my protecting him means preparing him. He will amount to nothing as a king if he does not earn some scrapes along the way. And the time is short, Miriam! The days will retreat so fast that it will seem as though we awake next Shabbat and his kingdom will be upon us. We must see that he is ready. Will you continue to contend with me that he had a short tussle with his cousin?"

"A short tussle!" Miriam burst. "Both the story and their wounds make it seem more like a brawl!"

Yosef could not help himself. He actually chuckled a little, which did not pacify Miriam in the least.

Regaining himself, "Too true, Dearest, too true. However, you must understand that when men really want to do violence to the other, their means are much meaner. Neither of the boys picked up stones or staffs. They had aggression to work out, yes, but there was no murder in their eyes. You'll see. Today you will wonder if they had even tangled yesterday."

Miriam sat with that for a moment before she asked, "How was Uncle about it all?"

Yosef laughed unrestrained. "He clenched his fists!"

"What!?" Miriam demanded.

"He may be old, my Lady, but he is still a man, and his son was in a scrap. We all quicken before battle."

Finally, at the peak of her frustrations, Miriam blurted, "Men are more stupid than antelopes locked at the horns!"

Without any hesitation, Yosef rejoined, "Perhaps we would not be so hot-headed if our women did not raise our blood so well!"

"Unbelievable..." said Miriam, as she hastened to leave Yosef in bed, not before tossing a pillow in his face.

But the quick-witted carpenter would not have it. Hastily, he grabbed her by the wrist and pulled her back close. And then he kissed her in all the places that she liked best. Miriam resisted for only a flash of an instant before she was most eagerly taken in, and responsive.

Breakfast would be delayed a while yet.

───────────────

The little brothers Ya'akov and Yose played at Marching Pegs on their tiny board in a corner of the living area. Yosef had whittled the set for the boys as a gift last Rosh Hashanah. He planned to sneak in a game with them later that evening.

Shlomit sat in his lap on the floor. Her tiny two-year-old body was content to cozy in her Abba's warmth. Yosef cherished these times. Long as the days might be, he knew the years were flying fast. His daughter's hair was too curly to hang down on its own and too short to weave into a single braid. Miriam did her best to pull her hair up into a few tight bundles at the top. Shlomit's eyes were still too big for her face, giving her the precious proportions of appearing to see everything even while naïve to the world. Yosef held her close and breathed in all of it. This little girl had his tzitziyot tied around her fingers.

Their morning had been as languorous as had been their walks to and from the synagogue. The early evening sun was descending upon the household as everyone chatted about the teachings from the synagogue. One particular passage from the parashah arrested their attention that week.

"Would you recite it for us again, Yehoshua?" Miriam asked.

The young messiah obeyed.

"Today Adonai your God commands you to do these statutes and ordinances. You shall therefore keep and do them with all your heart and with all your soul. You have declared today that Adonai is your God, and that you would walk in His ways, keep His statutes, His mitzvot, and His ordinances, and obey His voice. Adonai has declared today that you are a people for His own possession, as He has promised you, and that you should keep all His mitzvot. He will make you high above all nations that He has made, in praise, in name, and in honor; and that you may be a holy people to Adonai your God, as He has spoken."

They had been discussing the portion for at least an hour. Such promises always posed a difficulty for the Jews in their captivity to Rome. On the one hand, it was encouraging to be reminded of their national legacy within the schemes of HaShem. On the other hand, they were anything but high above all the nations. To imagine such a station in the world was so far from reality that it was disheartening to consider.

Zechariya spoke into the suspense hanging in the air. "Why do we suppose that Yisrael has not been lifted up?" He asked the question as a good sage would. He was too old and too studied not to have an opinion himself. But the emphasis was always upon repetition and reminder in their interactions. Torah was so vast, they needed each other to retain the immensity of its wisdom. And, like a good teacher, the wizened priest delighted to hear the thoughts of his fellow students even more than he took pleasure in talking at length.

Yosef always enjoyed watching the old man work a room.

"It is because we have not yet defeated the idolatrous Romans," blurted Yochanan.

"Is that so?" returned Zechariya.

"What else could it be, Abba?" rejoined Yochanan.

"Surely that is a possibility, my son, maybe even a likelihood," said Zechariya. "Do we have any other opinions before us?"

Yosef was satisfied with the response. It was difficult to consider anything more glaring than the disgrace of Roman idolatry as the worst blight upon the Land. He shuddered to remember the defilements of the Temple at the hands of Antiochus and Pompey. Even the women displayed the quiet consent of agreement, and they were never quick to celebrate so much as an implicit call to arms.

Then his thoughts turned to Gaius. They had exchanged their

knowing glances at the synagogue earlier that day, in what had become something of a silent ritual between them. The centurion had become the embodiment of the greatest inner turmoil in Yosef's understanding of the ways of HaShem.

The Gentile God-fearers became more and more prevalent in all of the synagogues with each passing year. In that way, it looked as though the Torah was beginning to become a light to the nations. On the other hand, the good carpenter could not help but resent, at least in part, that his own synagogue's ownership of several inestimable holy scrolls was due to the reverent generosity of these half-committed Gentiles.

If they were truly worshipful of HaShem, then why not take upon themselves the circumcision and the keeping of mitzvot? Yosef found it dissatisfying that they were intrigued while also being undevoted. A Jew risked much, every day, simply by getting up each morning to set out to keep and do the Torah once again.

His own sect, that of the Pharisees, risked the most in Yosef's estimation. They had not abandoned Yisrael, as the Essenes had done. Neither had they aligned themselves with the Herodians, as the Sadducees had done. No, the assumed position of the Pharisee, somewhere in between, neither departing nor assimilating, was an ongoing tension to preserve.

God-fearers risked much less, if anything at all. They carried the weight of the Roman government with them even if they did choose to demonstrate pretenses of submission in the synagogues. Yet, the studies that Yosef cherished, available right there where he lived, came to him through these Gentiles of questionable designation.

What's more, especially when it came to their centurion benefactor, Gaius, Yosef could never shake the feeling of... calling. He hesitated to admit the sensation to himself. There was always something striking in those unspoken acknowledgements between the two men. But what could the father of the messiah do with any of it? The centurion was a powerful man, wielding the sword of an empire that did not look kindly upon the Jews.

"Perhaps the enemies of Yisrael are not the enemies of Yisrael," said Yeshua.

Yosef was jostled from his ruminations as Yeshua spoke.

"What?!" said nearly everyone all at once, Yosef and Yochanan louder than anyone.

"How did the Romans come into our lands?" Yeshua responded without hesitation.

"How is that even a question!" demanded Yochanan.

Yosef did not voice it, but his face was as incredulous as Yochanan's words.

"If the matter is easy to dismiss, my son," interjected Zechariya, "then respond with something more substantive than your indignation. Yes?"

Yosef recollected himself at those words from the wise priest. So many times, the father of the messiah could not understand the mind of his son. He remembered how often his young scholar's understanding of Torah was leagues beyond his own. So, Yosef steadied himself again in patience as well as kindness. Thinking this was a much safer gathering than the general assembly in the synagogue, the good carpenter decided to restrain his impulses on the matter. Zechariya would do a fine job moderating the discourse. And as always, he couldn't help but wonder where Yeshua might lead the room throughout the discourse.

"All right," said Yochanan flatly. "Did the Romans not march into our Land with their abominations? What good is the question of their arrival?"

"'It is a land that Adonai your God cares for,'" Yeshua recited, "'the eyes of Adonai your God are always on it, from the beginning of the year up to the end of the year.' Did the eyes of HaShem waver so that the Romans might sneak past His watchful gaze?"

Yochanan was unresponsive though unconvinced; disagreement remained on his face.

"Yehoshua, do you think that HaShem, blessed is He, invited the Romans into Yisrael?" Zechariya challenged. The kindly priest had noticed Miriam's usage of her son's full name during Shabbat. He was quite pleased to acquiesce to her habit. "Are we to think that the Romans are long-lost brothers of the tribes of Yehudah? Or that HaShem would have us granting them tracts of land along the River Yarden? Would He restore Edom to forgotten birthrights?" Zechariya was didactically playful.

"Didn't Yisrael do the inviting, Uncle?" Yeshua responded.

"How dare you!" erupted Yochanan.

One stern look from Zechariya silenced the boy. Elisheva placed her hand on her son's head and stroked his hair for the duration of the discussion. If Yochanan minded the touch, he did not evidence it. He was like that stoic canine that never acknowledged affection but never turned away from it either. Elisheva delighted in having a son with such hair to care for.

"Come, Yehoshua. How did we welcome the Romans into Yisrael?" Zechariya prodded, unperturbed yet to the point.

"Did we not give them access to our Land when we formed an alliance with them, Uncle?" Yeshua replied.

"No, the Sadducees did that when they aligned themselves with that scoundrel, Herod!" said Yochanan. His mother's hand was still upon him. There was no kindness in his voice, but he was composed. Zechariya let the rebuttal stand undeflected.

"No, Yani," responded Yeshua. "Herod was little more than a fox that the Sadducees solicited to help them outsmart the wolves that we had lured. The Maccabees formed that alliance with the Romans before Herod was even heard of."

The history was in everyone's keeping. They were all educated, all of them well studied. However, that challenge to the legitimacy of the

Maccabees had not occurred to anyone, not even Zechariya. Every year, all Yisrael celebrated the victory of their champion, Yehudah the Hammer, and the eight-day-miracle of the menorah lights. That the Maccabee brothers saved Yisrael and rededicated the Temple was a tremendous victory to celebrate. The household had not considered that the Maccabean clan had erred in their governorship.

"'Five of you will chase one hundred and one hundred will chase ten thousand,'" Yeshua continued.

"Yisrael has never wanted for alliances. It has only ever erred in obedience. Our Father is a Faithful Companion, blessed is He, but He will not force Yisrael into covenant faithfulness. That is only for Yisrael to fulfill. Until that time, He chastises His people as a father to his sons. Yisrael's discipline is the consequence of its own sins."

No one had any rebuttals or challenges. The statement was so convicting that no one wanted any further development on the matter either. They sat in a contemplative silence together for the fleeting moments of Shabbat.

Yosef looked at his son as they were all prayerfully quiet together. Not for the last time, he wondered over himself at what kind of king Yeshua would become. The carpenter was surprised at how much more Yeshua had considered political rivalries and kingdom conquests than he had suspected. And Yosef was surprised at how steeped even those thoughts were in Torah oracles. Then he was surprised that he was surprised. This was Yeshua, after all. The boy was never anything less than a waking wonder.

For the first time in several months, for as long as Yosef had intended to have a final reckoning with his son about his impending kingship, he actually found his angst greatly alleviated. It was as though the grain of a heavy timber had accidentally aligned itself with one of Yosef's builds. He did not understand how Yeshua came to such a deep and profound understanding of such things, because there were certainly no secret mentors involved in his life. Nevertheless, it was clear that the young messiah had come to an apprehension of the nations through nothing more than his life in study and prayer. What other wisdom did his son keep in hiding?

As the sun finally settled down into the night, Miriam called the household to the table once again. A stone pitcher of wine, an empty glass, an ornate box of spices, and the elegant burning candlesticks were set before them. Zechariya presided over the Havdalah.

"Behold, God is my salvation! I will trust and will not be afraid.

For the Lord, Adonai, is my strength and my song.

He also has become my salvation.

With joy you will draw water from the wells of salvation.

Blessed are You, Adonai, our God, King of the Universe,

Who creates the fruit of the vine."

The old priest lifted a stone pitcher and a lone glass from the table and poured a serving of wine all the way to the brim, so perfectly that only a few single drops slipped over the edge and rolled down the side of the glass, dripping below and extinguishing the candle-flames. It was an impressive feat that nothing spilled. How steady his hands were! Every man attempted this demonstration in his own home at the Havdalah ceremony every week. Few were ever successful to replicate this image of bounty and offering before HaShem with such precision.

"Blessed are You Adonai, our God, King of the Universe,

Who creates the various spices."

Miriam held up the circular container, as wide as both of her hands spread out, as she slowly twisted a clever mechanism from the bottom. Yosef had concocted the design himself and took several months to refine it. The lid had a pomegranate carved into its surface. As Miriam spun the device open, what had at first appeared as a single piece of wood suddenly spread apart into six separate pieces that unfurled to the very outside of the container. Once fully opened, the box appeared like the star-shaped leaves of a pomegranate. It elicited a gasp from guests every single time they beheld it. Yosef possessed a craft to entrance kings.

The entire family took turns passing around the contraption and inhaling the many wonderful fragrances that had been hidden within the vessel. Yosef and Miriam had spent all their years together curating the aroma of their household. Even as the family bade a reluctant farewell to Shabbat for yet another week, their pains were alleviated as their souls stirred before such invigorating delights.

"Blessed are You Adonai, our God, King of the Universe,
Who creates the lights of fire."

Yosef held another bit of work before everyone in the palm of his hand. It didn't look like much more than a very small block of wood, no bigger than a man's wrist. He placed it between both thumbs and middle fingers, pinching it in midair. Then, with a performer's flair and a father's showmanship, he smiled at the table right as he snapped both hands and sent the device spinning all the way above the height of his head, just skimming the ceiling. As soon as it was released from his grip, it spun out into a flurry of flickering lights. It was like the pops and cracks that a fireplace sometimes makes without warning, but a whole series of them strung together, end over end, as it elevated before the household's watchful, wondering witness. No sparks ever spread out upon the table or reached anyone's seat even as it flashed such a concentration of little lightning streaks that everyone thought they might catch some of them falling. This particular trick of his was one he never revealed to anyone.

"Teach much of what you know to anyone who will learn from you, Yeshua," the master carpenter would sometimes instruct his son during his apprenticeship, "but *never* teach anyone *everything* you know!" That last bit he would always pronounce with a wink and a grin. Yeshua beamed at the lesson every time.

Just as everyone caught their breath and squealed in enchantment, Yosef's little handheld hive of fireflies closed itself up as it descended back down from the height of its flight, and fell into his hands a simple blocky peg once more. The family roared in applause and begged for a repeat performance. The adults were just as insistent as the children.

Yosef held up his hands as though the wonder-peg had vanished of its own accord.

"Many wonders reveal themselves to us only once in our entire lives, children!" Yosef said with enthusiasm. He was still holding court. "That is why we must always be vigilant as Gid'on before battle. We never know how HaShem, blessed is He, might appear before our very eyes!"

Even though he addressed the children, he intended the brief lesson for the ears of the adults as well.

While everyone protested and pleaded for the display just one more time, Zechariya laughed and came to the aid of his old friend. He called for their attention, and they heeded him, even if with a few passing complaints.

"Blessed are You Adonai, our God, King of the Universe,
Who distinguishes between the holy and the secular."

Miriam once again offered the cup of blessing to Elisheva, who drank gratefully and returned it to her niece. The entire family lingered over their sips in turn as they passed the cup around the table. Zechariya was unhurried as the cup would arrive finally at his place at the table.

They had bidden farewell to Shabbat with all their senses. Even as they prepared for the onset of the new week, they could not help but to anticipate the next Shabbat. This was the foremost of their holy, set apart times.

"Shavua tov!" they all exclaimed.

8

A Man's True Home

"IF YOU WOULDN'T mind delaying your trip one more day, my friend, I could certainly use Yani's help in my build today," Yosef requested of Zechariya. "Besides, it looks to be a lively party tonight when Shlomo presents the pergola to his wife. I think that you and Elisheva would enjoy yourselves."

"Are you trying to bribe an old man with wine that you haven't purchased, you huckster?" Zechariya chided.

"Only if such a ploy would prove effective, most noble priest," Yosef returned. "Otherwise, I might take offense that you would question the honor of my motives."

"How good is the wine?" Zechariya inquired.

"Good enough for a blessing, my friend," Yosef grinned, "perhaps several if our host becomes generous!"

The men laughed as they plotted. Zechariya had no intention of departing any sooner than he had to. He was glad for this gracious pretense on the part of Yosef. The two men understood each other very well. They were as brothers born into different tribes.

"I'll tell you the scheme, old friend," Yosef began. "Very soon Shlomo's wife, Tamar, will join Miriam for breakfast. Having Elisheva at hand as another hostess will ensure us the diversion that we need. Shlomo has made the space ready for us to erect the pergola at their estate. Yeshua and I have already tested the joinery. All we need is the time to set everything in the ground and make ready for the party."

"All well and good, Yosef," said Zechariya. "At what point do I set to work on the wine?"

Yosef slapped the old priest on the back. "As soon as we can prevail upon the host, you old blesser."

The previous night, right after Shabbat had come to an end, the men had loaded the cart with all of the timbers and various components for the next day's build. Yosef was resolute in his observance of Shabbat, and he was necessarily industrious in his labors, too. Most every week, very soon after the sun had set and the family had prayed Havdalah, the master carpenter was setting himself back to his labors.

They would not harness Shimshon to the cart until he had both eaten his breakfast and relieved himself. One morning months ago, soon after purchasing the donkey, Yosef set off hastily into the day. He had fed the front end of the creature and allowed him his time, but had not waited for the business end of the beast to conduct its affairs. After harnessing the animal to his load for the day, they had not gotten so much as a mule's kick down the road before all of Shimmy's viscous contents were dispersed all over Yosef's wooden payload. It was one of Yosef's best virtues that he had learned to govern his temper. Nevertheless, that morning tested his mettle.

The only solution the master carpenter could contrive on the fly was rather repugnant, but it was the best awful idea that he found practicable. He could not very well just remove the refuse as the mottled stains would remain unseemly. Paring and sanding wouldn't do because that would only establish bright brindling against the semi-aged surface of the wood. No... the father of the messiah had to humble himself to the willingness to collect Shimshon's draff raffle... and work it into every surface of every timber... and then he had to wipe clean every surface thereafter. Only this protracted and pungent drudgery would deliver a consistent and (counter-intuitively) an attractive finish to the wooden members once they were so treated.

It was Yosef's good fortune that only one neighbor witnessed the detritus drama. It was Yosef's bad fortune that said neighbor forever after referred to Shimshon as "the carpenter's painter." Had the memory not embedded itself indelibly within his nostrils, Yosef might have allowed the quip to imbue the event with humor. But it did, so he didn't.

He did, however, always retain the wisdom from that ordeal. Yosef was usually far-seeing enough to avoid calamity. On the occasions in which he was not, he rarely had to learn the same lesson twice. "Let's not rush ourselves into hiring the donkey to do our lacquer," he would sometimes say to Yeshua, to which the young messiah would always scrunch up the whole of his face as he let slip a rueful laugh.

Miriam and Elisheva awaited Tamar's arrival as the men began to set off. Just before the "Go" order, Yosef placed a broad cloak atop Shimshon's haunches. He paid all requisite respects to the unpredictability of his brute's undesirables. And then his heart sank as that familiar voice rang out from across the street.

"Hey, Yosef! Do all your painters wear their cloaks below their waists?" the neighbor called out.

Zechariya knew the sound of a gibe when he heard one, but he had no context for the jest. He turned around with a face full of light, already eager to hear either the story or the next string of taunts. Old men always made time for absurdity, all the more so with strangers.

Yosef was uncharacteristically gruff with the wizened priest. He grabbed him by the elbow, started walking and said, "Come, come!" His olfactory was reminding him of things that he had not yet learned how to laugh about.

With four downward drumming tweets of his whistle, Yosef gave Shimshon the order to march. So long as he was fed and rested, the donkey was always responsive. It was just too bad that the neighbor wasn't as impressed with the carpenter's fine training of the animal as he was with the animal's once-grand inconvenience upon the carpenter.

As they began the trek to Shlomo's house, Zechariya looked at Yosef perplexed, which Yosef ignored altogether. Behind them, the carpenter could just barely overhear Yeshua murmuring to Yochanan, after which both of the boys fought their stitches for the rest of the way. Of course, Zechariya continued to look to Yosef for some explanation, but the carpenter would not soon dignify the silent query with a response. He dreadfully hoped that this would not be the shape of the entire day as he wrinkled his nose and harrumphed a little huff.

———————

The route uphill to the blacksmith's residence was a circuitous one. Natzeret was so jagged that the path conducive to a laden cart and a donkey wound all throughout the village. Whenever the women drew water from the fountain spring at the bottom of their community, the mood and demands of the day determined whether a lady would choose the faster, more excruciating climb, or the slower, more walkable snaking trail.

They made it to Shlomo's estate relatively unscathed. Zechariya had desisted with his inquiring glances. The boys had mostly ceased their snickering. Yosef had almost forgotten certain odors. Shimshon's cloak remained unsoiled, although the carpenter unharnessed him with all due haste.

"Yosef!" Shlomo bellowed. "So good to see you, my friend!" The giant forge of a man approached them with big, boisterous energy. His bulk never failed to afflict the senses. It was impossible to simply become habituated to the hulk.

"Good morning, Shlomo," Yosef returned. He greeted the blacksmith in warmth, even though he remained a little suspicious of the large man.

"What fine company have you brought with you today?" Shlomo asked.

"Shlomo," Yosef responded, "this is Miriam's uncle, Zechariya of the Tribe of Levi, wise priest and an even better friend. You'll never want for a man with greater insights – or greater escapes. He has gotten me out of more binds than I care to admit."

"A Levite!" exclaimed Shlomo. "I like him better already! The blessings come free of charge, don't they?"

"Most certainly, my lad," smiled Zechariya, "they most certainly do. Although, I must tell you, I have noticed over the years that my memory and my enunciations have a tendency to improve in their quality of blessing once I have had a proper vintage in hand."

"We are going to get along great," Shlomo laughed as he grasped the old man's hands, nearly enveloping Zechariya's forearms in the girth of his blacksmith's grip.

"And this," continued Yosef, "is his son, Yochanan. He is a mighty lad bound for great things. HaShem, blessed is He, keeps a close eye on this one."

"Hello, boy!" said Shlomo.

"Good morning, sir," returned Yochanan.

"Of course, I remember this one," ragged Shlomo, mussing Yeshua's hair.

The young messiah gave Shlomo his customary wordless grin during these interactions of theirs. It always bothered the blacksmith that he could not get a rise out of Yeshua. It never seemed to bother Yeshua that his hair got messed up as retaliation.

"All right, Yosef," Shlomo recovered, "where to begin?"

"We are constructing the pergola within the eruv, right?" Yosef confirmed.

"Yes indeed, absolutely!" said Shlomo. "Tamar will love it there, and of course the neighbors will appreciate it too."

Yosef had to admit to himself that he was surprised by the gesture.

To place the pergola within the shared community courtyard would mean that all of the neighbors had access to it. The father of the messiah was unsure whether this decision represented generosity or grandiosity on Shlomo's part, or some mixture of both. Then he chastised himself for presuming upon the blacksmith's motives. It was a good gift in a good place. That was sufficient for Yosef's purposes.

They wheeled the load around several houses until they came to an opening conducive for the haul, bringing the contents into the center of the enclosure. Yosef and Yeshua knew their items so well that they wordlessly began laying out the timbers according to their order of erection. Yochanan immediately fell into assisting with the burdens.

Then Shlomo began imposing himself. He was asking questions about everything, insisting that Yosef double-check his measurements before it was too late, scrutinizing and criticizing mortises and tenons that were not mated to each other. It was maddening.

Yosef knew that they would never get anything done with the lug hanging about, throwing his weight and nonsense around. Then it would somehow become the carpenter's fault that the build was not completed in time for the party. Yosef could not determine whether Shlomo was oblivious to his impositions or if this was another scheme concocted to haggle the price down at the end of the day when the carpenter "failed to deliver in timely fashion" or some such contrivance.

At one point, Shlomo placed himself squarely at the working end of Shimshon's mallet whackers. Yosef entertained the notion of letting one of his kick-whistles out into the air just so he could get some work done. Then he chastised himself for that, too. But the indecision between a one-leg or a two-legs whistle resounded in his imagination for a while regardless.

Nearly an hour had passed with such aggravations when Zechariya placed his hand inside one of Shlomo's massive trunks of an arm.

"Shlomo, would you mind taking an old man to see your smithy?"

Zechariya asked as if he were a child during Chanukah. "I have seen Yosef's trade so many times, and I have always wanted to see where a blacksmith performs his transformations."

The blacksmith seemed a little bit jarred at first, and then he swelled with enthusiasm.

"You three will be all right if we leave for a while, Yosef?" Shlomo asked as if he were somehow integral to the success of the construction.

"Oh, we will make do," Yosef answered. He did his very best not to light up in response.

Zechariya and Shlomo left the eruv and headed for the smithy, several minutes away. Just before they rounded the corner, Zechariya looked over his shoulder and gave a secret wink to Yosef. At the edge of earshot, Yosef could hear Shlomo's big laugh reverberating throughout the neighborhood. If the Chariot of Fire had descended that very moment to whisk Zechariya away from the Earth, Yosef would not have been surprised. He was a righteous man all the way from his woolly eyebrows to his massive soul.

"All right, boys," Yosef said, turning back toward the work. "We are shorter on time than I would like. Are you up for a little bit of risk-taking and derring-do today?"

Yeshua and Yochanan were good-spirited young men. They knew the value of hard work and good attitudes, and they showed it in their labors. Even so, the suggestion of a little play in their day was sufficient to motivate them even more.

"If you will promise me to mind your feet and keep your heads," Yosef continued, "and promise me even more not to breathe a word of our activities to your mothers, then we can tighten up our work and have some fun while we're at it."

That was all they needed to spend the day sweating and toiling like Ark-bearers in the Wilderness.

The completed pergola was superlative. Yosef performed his labors as an act of worship, honoring HaShem with every touch of chisel, saw and hammer. His work was always fervent.

Nevertheless, he was even more attentive to the design and execution of the pergola than his standard levels of excellence. Shlomo was paying some eight times more than he had anticipated for the structure. Therefore, Yosef intended to deliver no less than ten times better than his expectations. Seeing it stand proud and ornate, unlike any other of its kind, the master carpenter was certain that there would be no hard feelings on the matter. The blacksmith might even think that he had gotten the better end of the bargain, which was, of course, what the father of the messiah wanted as a result in all of his dealings.

Rather than a staggered arrangement of flat level joists and opposite laid battens, Yosef had designed the rafters within a six-sided hip layout. The hips and rafters were framed in precise curvatures so that the roof of the pergola swelled and keeled from the top to the bottom in perfect rolling arcs. It looked like an enormous crown sitting atop a giant's table. A body would feel like royalty simply by sitting beneath its shade. No one had ever seen anything like it. The carpenter knew his craft.

The posts were also hexagonal, perfect in their symmetry. Chiseled into the fascia of the posts was the most ornate scrolling inlay of many vines winding their way from the ground to the beams. Yosef and Yeshua had taken the time not only to carve them beautifully, they had also burned the carvings meticulously so that the design stood out a deep dark against the bright hue of the cedar. When the pergola aged and turned gray, the carvings would retain their contrast. What's more, even after real live vines would grow their way to the top and cover the roof, the contrast would continue to serve as a backdrop, creating the illusion of extra depth and shadow. The design was so well thought out that it would only continue to improve with age.

To his credit, Shlomo had done a fine job planning a surprise party for his wife. This was their twentieth wedding anniversary. He wanted to see Tamar elated.

Food and drink had been arranged. Musicians arrived early to set up. Neighbors joined together to make the courtyard festive.

Guests began arriving with their contributions and gifts. Shlomo was much to endure at times, but he was a member in good standing within his community nonetheless. Nearly all the families from the synagogue would be in attendance besides many of Shlomo's associates from Sepphoris. If Tamar would be disappointed with anything, it could not be the feeling of a small party.

The blacksmith had centered himself beneath the pergola awaiting Tamar's arrival. He had no complaints or criticisms for Yosef, but it soon became clear that Shlomo's final satisfaction was contingent on his wife's reaction. Which, truth be told, that bothered the good carpenter none whatsoever, as he knew that Tamar's sense was more reliable than Shlomo's. Yosef worried less and bided his time.

All assembled came to a hush as one of the young lookouts gave them the alarm that the ladies were coming down the street. Miriam and Elisheva had done a splendid job distracting Tamar all day. Now the moment had come.

As the three ladies entered the eruv, the three little children tucked within their gaits, Tamar was confused for just the slightest instant before everyone erupted in surprise. She jolted, then she laughed freely, euphoric about the ruse and its revelation. In many ways, Tamar was something of a perfect woman to celebrate with such a gathering. She had been the talk of the town all those years ago when her father entertained suitors on her behalf. With the most minimal of head coverings, her dark hair sprawled like midnight and her eyes glittered like emeralds. She was enchanting by all accounts and her expressiveness matched her elegance. Any emotion she felt showed full on her face. No one had to guess how happy she was on an evening like this one.

Thereupon she saw the pergola. She was so frozen that for a moment she seemed disappointed. Then Tamar noticed Shlomo beneath the canopy, waiting for her to join him with his arms outstretched in her direction. Without hesitation, she glided toward her husband.

The woman was so graceful in her promenade that one might think she had rehearsed this moment before. As she approached the pergola, her eyes broke away from Shlomo just briefly enough to admire the ornateness of the structure. The next instant she was fixated once again on her husband. Upon her last step toward Shlomo, Tamar leapt into the air and threw her arms around his neck, whereupon the mighty blacksmith caught his wife and held her close, her legs dangling almost to the height of his knees.

Everyone broke out into cheers and congratulations as husband and wife kissed beneath the pergola. The gathering had the good sense to leave the two alone for a time as the partiers helped themselves to the bounteous spread of good food and better wine. No one needed to be told how to enjoy themselves as the musicians set the mood for merriment.

Zechariya came to Yosef and clasped his hands, congratulating his fine build. Elisheva doted on him too. Then Yosef felt Miriam's arms hugging him from behind. Their daughter Shlomit clung to his legs within the embrace.

"I am always amazed to see your work completed," Miriam said. "And you must know..." she stood on her tippy-toes to whisper into Yosef's ear, "I am at least as proud to be the wife of the man who built it as Tamar is to be the wife of the man who purchased it."

After all the day's excitement, the father of the messiah was undone. He welled up at the sound of Miriam's affirmation. She never expressed any resentment to him about their lifestyle, but Yosef could not help but wonder if his wife had ever felt cheated by her allotment in life. Her respect and admiration were the foremost of his desires.

As if she could hear his thoughts, she made her meaning all the clearer.

"I have never for one day regretted being yours, nor having you as my own. You are a truly good man, Yosef – deeply, wholly good – and the very best of fathers in our home. No one else could have me as you do."

Yosef clasped her hands to his chest for a moment before he turned around to embrace Miriam face to face. They kissed. It may as well have been their anniversary.

After they had let their feelings resound in one another, Yosef observed that Shlomo and Tamar were still alone within the pergola. The blacksmith and his wife were taking in all of the details of the construct. There were so many that they were taken in by the artistry over and over again. They were also quite taken with each other.

The master carpenter whispered to Miriam, "perhaps I might impress you even more tonight, my Love." To which Miriam simply smiled. She did not know what to expect, but over the years she had come to appreciate her husband's penchant for flair.

Yosef waved to Yeshua and Yochanan, who of course had been standing together. They were quite obviously proud of themselves at the sight of everything. Tradesmen and their apprentices keenly cherished the full gratification of the recipients of their labors.

Having caught Yeshua's eye, Yosef merely nodded, to which Yeshua grinned and nodded back. Then he and Yochanan went to the far corner of the pergola, beyond the notice of Shlomo and Tamar. It was impressive how stealthy the boys knew how to be, the deftness in their movements.

Yochanan gave Yeshua a quick boost to climb up onto an overhanging rafter. Having surmounted, anchoring himself flat across the ledge, Yeshua then reached down to retrieve a very large bucket of water from his cousin. It was heavy, but they managed it well.

Yeshua hooked the handle of the bucket onto the same rafter

that he had climbed upon. Next, he stood up and established his footing in order to squat down and hoist up the bucket by the handle. Then he climbed to the top of the pergola, at the pinnacle of the crown, heavy bucket in arms. At last, Yeshua looked back to his father in readiness.

The party-goers were so occupied with themselves that no one had noticed the elaborate spectacle, which was perfect. Yosef lifted his voice above the crowd. The following moment required everyone's attention.

"Fellow Jews! Listen to my voice!" Yosef hollered. The din of the gathering came to a hush. Yosef was a well-respected man in the community. It was natural that everyone would heed him.

"My friends, I ask for only a moment of your time. Yeshua and I have a brief demonstration to make. If you would direct your attention to the pergola, you will see my faithful apprentice standing there, high and lifted up!"

Everyone did, and indeed he was. They noticed the deep bucket of water too. The same devilish scheme occurred to everyone at that moment. Miriam was aghast at what her husband and son were about to do.

Before Shlomo and Tamar could escape the pergola, Yeshua dumped all of the water out at the top of the crown. The party had already gone quiet, but there was a collective gasp as they all waited to see the unsuspecting husband and wife get soaked. It was a despicable stunt to pull at an anniversary.

Then, to everyone's unbelieving eyes, none of the water penetrated the lattice-work of the pergola's canopy. Daylight was clear through the top of the structure from every angle. It should not have shed water. Yet it did.

The blacksmith and his wife had ducked out of panic, but they remained dry. The master carpenter and his fine apprentice had staggered the battens up the graduation of the curved rafters so that there was just enough overhang from one layer to the next that the water rolled continuously downhill. Not a single drop landed beneath the covering of the pergola.

What's more, the water did not spill over the edges either. Yosef and Yeshua had also managed to conceal gutters within the cross-beams and downspouts within the posts. For several instants, one could hear the water moving but could not see it. Then suddenly all of the contents came spilling out of hidden wooden flaps at the bottom of the posts.

Shlomo and Tamar laughed as their three marriable daughters came rushing into the canopy to join them in their glee. The crowd cheered. They all clapped for Yosef and Yeshua. Miriam shook her head as she smiled at her husband. It was a marvelous trick.

Yeshua climbed down from the rafters, laughing and very pleased with himself. Yochanan had been waiting for him the entire time. They congratulated each other on their flawless execution of the caper. The little brothers, Ya'akov and Yose, joined the older boys in their enthusiasm, hoping to have a share in their glorious performance.

Then Yeshua waved to his father for permission, and Yosef inclined his head. They had planned this moment as well. Yeshua would offer a blessing over the couple.

The audience was looking at Yeshua as the rascal of the party. Their attention was his for the moment. He knew what to do.

"Thank you all for indulging our little demonstration," Yeshua said. The crowd gave another brief upsurge of applause. It had been a very good ruse.

"Truly, it delights us to have the work of our hands so well received. And none deserve it better than a husband and wife so well given to each other." Yeshua turned to look to Shlomo and Tamar in deference. He was standing only a few paces away from them, just at the edge of the pergola.

"However," Yeshua wavered, "what you should know is that there was a time when the good fellow Shlomo here had come to consider cancelling his order with my father!"

There was a brief murmur of surprise. What was the boy up to? Yosef had not expected this turn, and the two of them had planned this moment together.

"It was an interesting day," Yeshua resumed. "Have you ever seen two Jews in disagreement over the price?"

They all laughed, except for Yosef, Miriam, Tamar and Shlomo. The two women held their composure, waiting to see what came next. Yosef and Shlomo were both red in the face, for different reasons and with different emotions. The blacksmith's lovely daughters giggled to each other freely. They knew their father well and were not embarrassed by the account.

"I tell you truly," Yeshua spoke over the babel. "I was called to act as their witness that day. It seemed as if they might never speak to one another again. During the worst of it, Shlomo had determined to take the sum allotted for the pergola and go traveling with his wife instead." The young messiah gave the crowd a moment to murmur to each other.

"Obviously, everything worked out, as we are all gathered here to celebrate them. Nevertheless, I learned an invaluable lesson that day, one that I had learned from watching my Abba over the years, an impression that I had received from him, although the imprint lacked words within me until that moment in Shlomo's smithy. The reason that Shlomo could be flippant about the pergola was because he was resolute about Tamar. Of course, he could travel with her instead of acquire something for her. Because the deepest truth that I realized that day was this: that a man is only home in the companionship of his wife. Now I bear witness before you today, that Shlomo is such a man and his wife Tamar is such a lady. Would that HaShem, blessed is He, allot all of their years together in joy with one another."

And just like that, Yeshua had inverted his moment of scandal into a romance to be sought after. Yosef and Miriam chuckled together as they caught their breath. Shlomo and Tamar embraced and kissed yet another time; their daughters made a family-wide embrace with them. All in attendance cherished the moment with their companions.

Yosef beheld Shlomo and Tamar beneath the pergola and saw it anew, as though it were the covering of their wedding chuppah. He wondered whether the blacksmith had wanted that imagery all along but didn't know how to express it, or lacked the courage to say so. The good carpenter found himself suddenly endeared to the fellow with a newfound feeling of brotherhood coming over him. Shlomo was a lug, but he was their lug. And he was a pretty decent lug when all was said and done.

As wondrous and intimate as the quiet had become, the father of the messiah remembered their occasion. This was a party, after all. Yosef began to sing and the entire gathering joined him in the song.

"Blessed is everyone who fears Adonai,
    who walks in His ways.
For you will eat the labor of your hands,
    you will be happy, and it will be well with you.
Your wife will be as a fruitful vine
    in the innermost parts of your house,
your children like olive plants
    around your table.
Behold that so will a man who fears Adonai be blessed.
May Adonai bless you out of Zion,
    and may you see the good of Yerushalayim
    all the days of your life.
Yes, may you see your children's children.
Shalom be upon Yisrael!"

9

Treachery and Peril

THE FOLLOWING MORNING, Yosef roused himself with no small amount of regret. It had been a very good party, so it was going to be a very difficult day to begin. No one was forcing him out of bed but himself, a rule that he had imposed on his own person years prior. If he couldn't handle his wine the following day then he had no business handling it the night before. He groaned as he grinned and grimaced. It had been a very good party.

As was his custom, Yeshua was already up, wrapped in his tefillin and tallit, studying his Torah scroll. Shimshon had already been fed. The carpenter would not have to wait for either his apprentice or his donkey to be prepared for the day. He had only himself to get ready.

Father and son stole away quietly into the jagged straits of Natzeret with the donkey, intending to let the rest of the family sleep off their late night. Yosef and Yeshua both were glad to think of Zechariya, Elisheva and Yochanan being with them for at least another day. They would be unlikely to depart for their long trip with a late start. The thought of returning home to them at least once more that evening was a happy expectation.

Shimshon was saddled with two full bags of tools. There were certain implements better left in the workshop. But the two men could carry much of their trade with them in their portable apparatus.

"Do we have another job to begin, Abba?" Yeshua asked.

"Not yet, son," Yosef answered as he touched the cedar chip behind his ear, making sure his carpenter's designation was apparent. "We're going to find work or we're going to make work. Another commission, a set of repairs, whatever we can manage. The first thing is for us to get out there and find out who's looking for us. They may not know they need us yet! So, we're going to attract their attention. Perhaps we will cross the valley north into Sepphoris in the search for our next customer."

They would make a good day of it. Even if they did not find work right away, they would be seen looking for it. And that would generate awareness to their availability. Anyone that needed a reminder about the master carpenter and his skilled apprentice would soon have it. Their town was not so large that they could be forgotten for long. Especially with the extraordinary spectacle of the pergola at hand, they should find themselves very sought after.

However, little did Yosef know this would become the hardest day ever since his family's narrow escape from Herod's mass infanticide over a decade ago. He would pay the debt of his decisions down with trauma thereafter. The toll would not be his fault, but he would bear the responsibility nonetheless.

No sooner had they come to the pinnacle of town than Yosef heard the shout that every Israelite dreaded, the voice of a Roman soldier.

"Jew! With the donkey! Halt!" commanded the soldier.

There was nothing for it but to comply. Yosef did not know what to expect, but he braced for the interrogation. It might only turn into a bit of harassment to endure. The Romans enjoyed their sport and they were bored far too often.

The soldier closed the distance and looked them both over for a moment, studying Yeshua with disturbing eyes. He stood closer than was courteous. He was taller than Yosef, an effect exaggerated by the long spear held even taller. The Roman enjoyed the intimidation of his weaponry.

After a few moments of this silent assessment, the soldier spoke.

"My armor. One mile. You carry."

Yosef's Greek was passable. He understood better than he could speak. More importantly, he knew the law.

"I agree," said Yosef. It was the best word that he could recall on the spot.

"Not a request, Jew," spat the Roman. He was already removing his armor and dropping it discourteously at the carpenter's feet. "For the next mile, you are my slave. I'll make you my prisoner if you err."

The father of the messiah could see right away that there was no point in trying to explain himself. This could only be unpleasant at best. The fewer words, the better. Yosef nodded and began picking up the armor, stacking it as well as he could for the long haul. Shimshon was already carrying near the limit of his load. The carpenter would not injure his donkey simply because the Roman had insulted his pride.

Yosef reached into one of Shimshon's saddlebags and pulled out a neat bundle of rope.

"What are you doing?" demanded the soldier.

"Rope – armor," said Yosef. "Better I carry."

"No time, Jew," the Roman refused. "Pick it up and march."

Through it all, Yeshua simply looked on. It was better that he remained silent. Yosef could see his concern. The two of them knew the only way through this imposition. They would endure it and hope that it was nothing more than an inconvenience. But they would be very wrong in that hope.

The three men and the donkey set off back down the slopes of Natzeret, leaving the township behind in about half an hour. It was slow going, with both Yosef and Shimshon carrying full capacity. They took the longer meandering path around all of the worst traverses. Townspeople looked on in bystanders' helplessness. Their best days were in the shadow of the Empire; their worst days were beneath its heel.

The armor was heavy in Yosef's arms. The best that he could do was to keep everything stacked on top of the interior of the long shield, with his arms spread outside the metal boss at the center of its surface. It was not meant to be carried but worn. There was no easy way to adjust it, no handy way to arrange things. As much as Yosef was managing the weight, he was also struggling to keep everything balanced. He would not allow himself to discover what happened if something dropped to the ground.

The sun was beating hot. Yeshua led Shimmy at the front. Yosef followed behind the donkey. The soldier menaced from the rear, the reminder of sword and spear close on the two Jews.

This was a miserable task with no chance of a rest. It was the longest mile Yosef had ever had to slog and trudge. Yet it was nothing in comparison to the mile that he would plow and hobble back on the other side of that same day.

"Today alone?" Yosef asked over his shoulder. He wasn't trying to make small talk. The carpenter did not understand how the soldier was on duty in isolation. They were not heading northwest toward the garrison but in the opposite direction. Yosef did not know a tremendous amount about the Roman Legions, but he was familiar enough with their patterns to know that this was highly irregular.

"Orders," the soldier flattened. "I do not discuss with a Jew; I only make him do my bidding."

The father of the messiah despised being humiliated in front of his son. He wondered what Yeshua thought of him throughout the forced march. Was he lessened in his son's eyes?

At one point, as if in answer to his thoughts, Yeshua grabbed the helmet from Yosef's load of armor burdens. It wasn't much of the weight, but the gesture meant everything to the downtrodden father. The transfer did not last long.

"Put that back!" the Roman barked. "One Jew's grime is enough to clean off of my equipment."

Yeshua complied and gave his Abba the briefest of conciliatory glances. In that moment, Yosef understood that they were fully together in this. They would have much to work out once the ordeal had passed, but the trust between them had not been disturbed. Father and son would endure this as one.

They passed through the pasture fields at the base of the town. Shepherds and herdsmen watched the regrettably common sight of a Jew walking before a Roman. Then they were in the desert wilderness of rolling hills with its rock jutted landscape and sparse grasses. Only a few wild carob trees dotted the sprawl of their footslog. The Romans had not constructed one of their immense roads near a small town like Natzeret, but even in the remote areas of Yisrael the Jews had preserved decent footpaths in their many annual sojourns to Yerushalayim.

Eventually, it dawned on Yosef that the soldier was not in any hurry at all. At no point had he demanded a brisker pace or complained about the slowness. There wasn't much energy for long thoughts beneath the strain, but the savvy carpenter realized that the Roman was enjoying the struggle that compounded upon his conscript. It could have been that the entire imposition was nothing but a show of strength. Maybe legionnaires were instructed to enforce these disruptions primarily as an intrusive, visceral reminder of the Empire's might. In any event, it was clear that the soldier took a sadistic pleasure in the carpenter's pains. Whatever the Roman's orders were, he was under no compulsion of time.

After what felt like an age in passage and a world in baggage, the soldier called for a halt. Apparently, they had arrived at their destination. None too soon, the carpenter thought.

Yosef had just begun to bend over and set his load down when he felt the heavy blow to the back of his head. The jolt of that sensation was like being stung, bitten and clubbed all at once. His eyes seared with a dank whiteness as everything below his neck went numb. He fell to his face immediately, his body crashing on top of the Roman's armor.

When Yosef looked up from the ground, his vision was blurry, and his head ached worse than the morning after a Purim festival. His son and the soldier were only a few paces ahead of where Yosef recollected himself in his stupor. But he could just make it out when the Roman lifted up his sword and bludgeoned Yeshua with the pommel right at the base of his neck.

"NO!" Yosef cried, in the very instant that Yeshua crumpled in the dirt.

It surprised the Roman to hear that Yosef was still alive. With sword and spear in each hand, he swung around to finish the job. The carpenter could not even see straight, and he felt his face getting wet with blood.

The speed with which everything occurred was too much to apprehend in the moment. It would be days and weeks of revisiting the disaster before Yosef had a somewhat clear recollection of the sequence of events. The ensuing calamity was a frenzy of instinct and desperation.

Shimshon had turned around toward the noise in a panic when the Roman's armor clattered and clanged beneath Yosef's plummet. As the donkey was facing Yosef, his hindquarters were pointed directly at the Roman, but only for the briefest window of opportunity. Had the carpenter been struck in the face, he would probably not have been able to execute his counterattack.

At the sound of two quick bursts of a single note from Yosef's sharp whistle, Shimmy kicked backwards with a solid leg. The donkey's hoof hit the Roman square in the stomach, which startled and hurt him, but only enough to enrage the soldier. As the legionnaire raised his sword to strike down upon Shimshon, the carpenter whistled one long shrill note that fell off all of a sudden. At the plummet of that note, Shimmy kicked backwards with both rear legs. It was enough to knock a full-grown man into last week, perhaps enough to kill him.

On the day that those dual powerful legs collided with a man's center, it folded him in half, and his sword and spear dropped use-lessly from his hands. Yosef wondered over the mechanics of it for a long time afterward, how the Roman did not go flying backward from the enormous blow, but there was no time for that curiosity in the moment. The carpenter watched as the Roman's top half pitched forward and his bottom half fell backward to the ground, his eyes and mouth gaping wide as he fought for air that he could not retrieve.

Once the soldier hit the ground, he was a writhing mess of agony, rolling from his back to his side to his back again, holding his stom-ach with both arms. He made no sounds other than that of his body thrashing. Eventually, he could force breaths through a labored wheeze; every inhalation sounded like a fight to the death.

For a moment heedless of the Roman, Yosef crawled through the sandy path toward Yeshua. He was motionless, but he was breath-ing. The father of the messiah could see where the blow had landed between his son's neck and shoulder. Nothing was broken. Yeshua would awaken with pains to last a couple of Shabbatot, but Yosef determined that he would be all right.

As they were still on a road subject to chance passersby, Yosef had to act quicker than the prophet Eliyahu in his flight from the wicked Queen Yezebel. Staggering up to his feet, he took the neat bundle of rope from Shimshon's saddlebags and bound the Roman's wrists together and then tied the lead to the donkey's harness. Yosef noticed a shack in a field on the east side of the road and pointed Shimshon in that direction. The carpenter stacked the soldier's armor on Shimshon's back and let out his "Go" whistle. The donkey marched, carrying the armor and dragging the soldier.

At last, Yosef placed Yeshua within the curvature of the Roman's shield and prepared to follow behind Shimshon. But then the father of the messiah noticed one of his tefillin on the ground. The thick leather strap had been severed right in the middle of the dense knot behind his skull. The back of Yosef's head was still oozing with blood, soaking his neck and running down his back, but bleary as he was, he understood why the soldier's blow had not ended him. The carpenter collected the tefillah that had saved him, hefted one end of the shield with Yeshua upon it, and pulled in the direction of the donkey.

From the moment of the first strike until the end of the anxious tug across the field, it had been only a few minutes in total, though they were enough to take years off of a man's life (nearly enough to take a man's life off the remainder of his years). Nevertheless, Yosef still had a torrent of terrible decisions to make. As horrendous as the ordeal had already been, the worst was ahead of him yet.

As soon as they got to the shack, the father of the messiah dropped the Roman on the opposite side of the road and tied him to the structure through the gaps in the vertical battens. He tied Shimshon to the shack as well, just in case he would wander and draw attention to their location. Yosef then laid Yeshua inside the shack itself, as comfortably as he could.

The good carpenter had never imagined himself into such a situation before. Suddenly he found himself with an insensible victim and a captive assailant, with an ensuing interrogation to perform. At last, he remembered his own bleeding.

It was an impressive gash, to be sure. Even grazing it brought the torture of light back to his vision. All in all, though, it was a manageable wound. For a moment he wondered at the protection that had been afforded him by his wearing of The Name. Then it occurred to him to repair the straps of his tefillah so that he could tuck a bandage between its purchase at the back of his head. The application was crude, but it would have to do.

Outside, the Roman still wheezed and groaned, but he collected himself in anger, as much as he could afford. He was almost insensate in his rage, which baffled Yosef. The soldier had assailed them without provocation. Yet, there he was still breathing, albeit laboriously, and the Roman was enraged as if he had somehow been wronged. Yosef's heart sank as he considered that he would be attempting to get words from an irrational beast.

"Bad soldier," said Yosef as he pointed to his slapdash dressing over the unfinished wound. "Lazy or stupid. I have no sword. Not dead. Bad soldier." Even through his stilted Greek, Yosef could see that the Roman took his meaning.

"You kill us," Yosef said. "I carry armor. No problems. Why the sword?"

The Roman only snarled in response. He didn't seem to have any fear of the carpenter. The soldier's face yielded nothing.

Yosef stomped the Roman's knees flat on the ground and stood upon them as he slapped him straight in the face – twice – as hard as he could with each palm. His tradesman's hands were quite suitable to the blows. The soldier was taken aback at the older man's strength; his eyes widened at the shock of being struck by a man he previously regarded as no kind of threat.

"Why the sword?" Yosef growled. Still, the Roman didn't answer.

The carpenter took a step back and looked the younger soldier over. Then the oddity occurred to him. The Roman had struck a death blow to himself but had only bludgeoned his son. The sequence did not make sense if murder had been the only agenda.

The realization was so revolting to Yosef that it took his mind a moment to catch up to what he already knew. They had not arrived in the proximity of this shack by accident. And the soldier never meant to kill Yeshua, at least not right away.

Yosef remembered the way that the Roman had looked them over in town. The soldier's lack of concern for expedience during the march coupled with his intention to make the carpenter weary. He knew the perverse appetites of the Romans.

In the thunderbolt of his realization, Yosef fell away from himself. At the brink of the unthinkable, primeval instinct overtook his

restraint. The protective impulses of a father dovetailed all too easily with the fury that had been kept in reserve during the many long
years of oppression, suddenly brought to the surface at the edge of a
sword. In the weeks to come, he would actually regret his actions on
that day. But at that moment, Yosef became undiluted action bent on
the singular purpose of protecting his own. Much later he would realize that if he had not left the sword and spear strapped to Shimmy's
saddlebags, had they been within reach right away, the Roman would
have been dead in an instant. As it was, with no weapons in hand, the
Roman was beaten instead, and it lasted much longer than an instant.

It didn't matter where Yosef hit him or where he kicked him so
long as his violence landed somewhere on the scoundrel's body. He
had become a man heedless, unhinged, pouring out his indignation
on the monster that would even so much as dream up the unconscionable against his son. Had anyone else witnessed the devastation,
they would not have been able to believe that it was Yosef doling out
the delirious brutality, not because he was regarded as a weak man,
but because he was reputed as such a composed man. But this day had
taken him beyond the constraints of temper.

"Mercy!" the Roman cried out. "Mercy! Mercy! Mercy!" And he
said it in Hebrew.

Then, suddenly, Yosef came to himself, his fists clenched and his
entire body rumbling like the earth beneath Egyptian chariots. He
found himself several paces away from the Roman, who remained
uninjured. The entire assault occurred in Yosef's mind. All of the rage
was present in his hands, but he had not spent it yet. Which left him
with a terrible decision to make.

"I know." Yosef was the one growling once again. "I know. You
want evil. My son."

It was a strange time to regret his lack of proficiency in Greek, but
he wished for better words nonetheless.

"What do I care what you know, Jew?" the Roman laughed. He

actually laughed! His speech was forced as his guts were still in turmoil, but he had regained some strength.

"Where do you think this goes? Would you kill me out here? Everyone saw us leave together. You are powerless against me. Whether you kill me or not, you are a dead man. Then your son. And your wife. How many children do you have? My centuria will make sport with all of them before your family is crucified. Maybe your entire dung heap of a village hangs from crosses as an example. You will wish that you had died back on the road."

It was sickening to hear such horrid predictions ring like truth, but Yosef knew the soldier was right. He did everything that he was supposed to do and he had become trapped regardless. Whether he killed the Roman or released him, the results would be the same. This had become an impossible impasse.

Then Yosef recalled one of the grimmer stories of his people – the day that two of the sons of Ya'akov wreaked havoc on an entire city. It was not a day they celebrated, but they remembered. In all things, the Jews remembered. Yosef puzzled over his predicament for what seemed like an age, but it came to a point where he simply had to act. He had to make a decision, even if it was nothing better than the best bad course of action that he could hatch.

His ill-conceived tactic, even at an imaginative level, was treacherous and none too inspiring. However, venturing the unexplored, Yosef concluded that the soldier would have to develop habits of concealment and subterfuge in his lifetime of visits to the Roman bathhouses. And if he ever thought to bring vengeance to Yosef's person or household, the carpenter could expose the soldier as a convert, which would call any accusation into question in the eyes of his superiors. Yosef had to imagine that the mere threat of humiliation would become its own permanent deterrent.

The carpenter went to Shimshon and stopped for just a brief moment. He looked at the sword and the spear and considered his options one last time. Then he reached into one of the saddlebags and retrieved a modest, slender knife. Yosef took care of all his tools. His knife was always sharp, although he never imagined its impending application.

"Dead Roman," Yosef said, "big problem. Roman not here, same problem. The Roman is right. I have a bad day."

"That's right, Jew-rat!" the Roman spat. "This has become the worst day of your life. You think your tiny knife will change anything? Kill me or don't. Your clan will suffer all the same."

"I think..." Yosef struggled to find the words in Greek. "I think... bad day for me, bad day for you. You cut me, I cut you."

Once again, the Roman sneered. Yosef wished that he could explain the fullness of his intentions, but the language barrier was too great to cross. He released what meager words he had in his keeping, then he hoped that his predictions and calculations would not be worse than the reality that had already been set before him.

"I make the Roman a Jew," Yosef said.

"What?!" exclaimed the soldier. His surprise was even greater than his anger had been. He was completely astonished at the suggestion. "You think you can make me worship your weak desert god? What good has your deity been to your degenerate, sniveling, mule-scum race of a people? I would rather die proud before I humiliated myself and became like one of you."

"I make the Roman a Jew," Yosef repeated. "Down here," Yosef pointed.

At last, the soldier looked horrified. Perhaps he didn't understand everything, but he understood enough. For most men, there were considerations far worse than death to entertain.

"YOU WOULDN'T DARE!" the Roman burst. He still lacked the strength to scream or yell, but he tried.

"Roman you take bad story home," Yosef said. "Alone on street. Sword and spear. Armor I carry. Old man and donkey. Knife. I make the Roman a Jew. Down here. Bad story. Bad day for me, bad day for you. Bad story. I make the Roman a Jew."

Yosef wished that he could simply say, "No one will believe your story." But it would have to do. The explanation didn't matter so much as the plan. And the potential outcomes were already bleak anyhow. If only it were as simple as burying the Roman and escaping with his own family. But one garrison would soon signal another. Their chances were slim. Yosef took a breath and set himself to the task.

He tied the soldier's feet to a stake in the ground and stretched him out. The Roman was impotent to fight back in any way, bound at hands and feet, tethered as if for a pagan sacrifice. And the precision of the upcoming removal was everything. As badly as Yosef wanted to murder the Roman and be done with it, he could not maim him if there was going to be any hope of this crazy gambit succeeding once they all returned. The carpenter wound some of the rope into a knot the size of his wrist and presented it to the soldier's mouth.

"Mouth," said Yosef.

The Roman looked imperious. He did not open his mouth. The carpenter slapped his throat, provoking a cough, then shoved the rope behind his teeth.

"Slow," Yosef said. "Danger. Bad cut or..." with a face expressing all manner of concern, "or more bad cut. Roman you choose."

Then Yosef performed the task he had never once imagined performing upon an unwilling convert. He knew the methods, but this was not how it was supposed to be. Considering everything, the carpenter was unbelievably gentle. Considering everything else, the soldier was impressively still. His body was rigid, locked and frozen in pain not to be welcomed without good reason. The Roman lacked that good reason, but he had retained enough good sense not to make a bad stroke worse. For the duration of the excision, they had become temporary allies. Neither of them wanted to see more removed than had been implied.

The act was grim. The scheme was insane. It was desperate and foolhardy and a wild gamble. It was the best that Yosef could do.

10

Qualms and Consequences

FOR THE FIRST time in Yosef's life, he was halfway home and hoping that the distance was farther to go. Disburdened of the Roman's armor for the return trip, the father of the messiah had never felt heavier. He had already cast his lots; there was no taking them back. If only he could prolong the amount of time until he had to watch them land.

Before they had left the shack, Yosef rigged a simple frame from the loose lumber and hitched it to Shimshon's harness. He lashed the long shield to that frame and laid the soldier upon it, donned in his armor once again. The saddlebags Yosef placed between the Roman's legs.

Yeshua rode on Shimmy's back, leaning upon his neck, in and out of sleep for the trip homeward. The donkey dragged the shield-frame behind them, laden with the soldier and the gear, heavy enough to leave furrows in the ground. Yosef carried the spear in hand and the sword and scabbard in his belt.

Whenever Shimshon needed a break, they stopped. Yosef had no mind to hurry the creature, for the donkey's well-being as well as his own state of mind. It had become clear that they would arrive at Natzeret around dusk. The carpenter could not determine whether daylight or darkness was better for what came next. His strategy was so outlandish, Heaven only knew what might occur.

In what might have been his last hour as a free man, Yosef prayed everything he could think to pray. He repented of all of his sins, known and unknown, and asked forgiveness. He sought the favor of HaShem for his family. He begged Adonai's help in the matter.

"Blessed are You, Adonai, the True Judge," Yosef said aloud.

Was Yeshua really the messiah? Their family had survived so much, it was implausible not to see the care and protection of HaShem over their story. Yet, there they were, a disheveled assortment of injured stragglers defying rationale: a man gashed within a knot's depth of death, a boy beaten senseless, and a reluctantly circumcised Roman soldier. Not to mention the donkey victorious in combat.

How could it be that HaShem would allow the messiah to be struck down? He Who sits above the heavens did not owe Yosef an audience, but what was the carpenter supposed to think on the bleak side of eternity? Prophecies and promises wouldn't amount to much if all of the intended heirs and recipients were exterminated.

On that dreadful day, Yosef traversed through the farthest recesses of his spirit as he trekked that lonely darkening road. He was a faithful man, one who had long ago become defined by his observance of the mitzvot. The carpenter was proud to be a Jew, a son of the covenant, even in spite of his people's persecution. But when the world became chaos and the Author of all things did not sign His Name legibly, the man could not help but question the veracity of the story.

Whenever faith loses hope it tests love. And there would be times when that love could only be proven through a white-knuckled surrender of the forlorn, in a grim devotion of desperation. Those abysmal chasms of hopeless faith would be the only means to prove out a steadfastness that outstrips the winds, a soul more inextinguishable than the sun, and the unfathomable depths of a love that delves deeper than the grave.

Yosef did not understand. He could not even pretend to begin to understand. But he would relent.

If this would become his last day, he would fill it with all the glory he could gather. His prospects had not improved any, but his resolve had become adamant. He found himself ready to sing.

"God takes His stand
  in the assembly of God.
He judges among the gods:
'How long will you judge unjustly
  and show partiality to the wicked?
Give justice to the poor and fatherless.
  Be just to the afflicted and destitute.
Rescue the weak and needy.
  Deliver them out of the hand of the wicked.
They know nothing;
  they understand nothing –
  they walk about in darkness.
All of earth's foundations are shaken.
I said: "You are gods,
  and you are all sons of Elyon,
yet you will die like men,
  and will fall like any of the princes."'
Arise, O God, judge the earth!
For You possess all the nations."

Yosef became heartened enough to catch the lots that he had cast. And he enjoyed a sardonic element of satisfaction to hear the Roman groan in his suffering. Perhaps the singing made it worse for the soldier, which didn't upset the carpenter in the least.

Yeshua became alert as well. He continued to lean upon Shimmy's neck, but he turned his face toward his Abba and smiled. And that was all that it took for all to be made well in Yosef's world once again.

"It feels like I missed some excitement," Yeshua grimaced.

"Indeed, son" Yosef smiled. "It's good to see you alert. How do you feel?"

"About like you'd imagine, Abba," Yeshua quipped. "How about the Roman?"

"Oh…" Yosef was not prepared to disclose everything to his son just yet. "He has been diminished somewhat, but he is still with us."

"Are we in for another adventure, Abba?" Yeshua searched.

"I will tell you this much for now," Yosef replied. "If we get through this all right, there is a talk that we must have right away. I've been giving you space for months, but I can't put it off any more!"

"That's fine, Abba," Yeshua replied. "It can't be any worse than this headache."

Yosef chortled at that. Yeshua chuckled as much as his neck could sustain it. If they were going to die, they would at least do it laughing together.

By the time they had made it to the outskirts of town, Yosef steadied himself for the winding ascent through the town. He had no idea what to anticipate upon their return. Even though he had strengthened himself, he had not become foolish as to their predicament.

The good carpenter had meant to sneak home and prepare his family for the difficulties before them. He thought perhaps to send his people away with Zechariya's family under the cover of darkness. There was a better chance of an old man and his clan being able to travel along the roads back to the Essenes, undisturbed by happenstance authorities, if Yosef were not in their party. If anything went afoul, he would be the primary suspect after all. In the meantime, he could finalize his schemes in a bit of plotting with Rabbi Nechemyah.

Alas. The father of the messiah was in for another surprise, and not even the last one for the night. His test was not yet complete.

When he turned the corner of the last switchback for the final approach up his familiar path, his heart sank down to the fringes of his tallit. Standing before the door of his home was a full unit of eight Roman soldiers, dressed in complete armor and weaponry. Gaius stood at their head.

Yosef hardly led the donkey into the street with his dual loads before Gaius saw him. Instantly, the carpenter knew there could be no delay. Escape was impossible. He could only guess the well-being of his family inside their home. This was not the situation that Yosef had anticipated.

The centurion didn't move, didn't give any orders, didn't do anything other than observe the Jew walking up the street with a boy on top of his donkey and an unusual load being dragged behind. His thoughts were as indecipherable as ancient manuscripts, as impenetrable as a Roman shield-wall. Then the centurion observed the spear in Yosef's hand.

Yosef held the man's gaze, not knowing what else to do. How was he supposed to hold a spear in any way that did not seem threatening? The father of the messiah took as deep a breath as he could without drawing attention to the fact that he was taking as deep a breath as he could.

The carpenter was decent with a sword but not much account with a spear. Nevertheless, when he considered the impending confrontation, he thought of the length of the weapon and what he might do with it in the imminent charge. Perhaps he would keep the bulk of the soldiers at bay with the spear before several rushed upon him. The sword was ready to be drawn once he dropped the spear. Maybe he could coax the donkey to kick a few more of the devils. Such thoughts and preparations ran through his mind as he maintained a lackadaisical pace, walking home as if it were any other night, and there just happened to be Roman soldiers at his door.

Then, as Yosef had but one last moment to prepare, Gaius turned and addressed his troops. Yosef knew nothing of Latin, so the terse orders were lost on him. But the very instant the centurion spoke, the unit of soldiers broke away in the opposite direction, bounding up the steep stone steps and away from the carpenter's home.

Only Gaius remained, with his left hand resting casually upon the hilt of his sword and his right arm hung nonchalant at his side. The man was all confidence and command. Motionless, inviolable in his stature of strength, he looked like one of the Roman's statues carved from stone and set high upon their pedestals. The wind was still so that not even his cape swayed. Even in the full darkness of night then upon them, the crimson crest of his helmet's plume stood out proudly against the backdrop of the looming sky. Despite his shaven face, the man was a mask of intimidation. His hooked nose looked like a sleek weapon beneath his brow. The centurion did not need a cadre to be daunting. He was the embodiment of the Empire.

While only a few paces away, Yosef lifted the spear slowly upright. Since the Roman did not communicate hostility, the carpenter would not either. It seemed more appropriate to point the spear away from his... what was he? An inquisitor, an adversary... an executioner?

Through it all, Yeshua remained still, leaning upon Shimmy's neck. Yosef did not address him in any way. He wondered how quickly he might unfasten the ropes to the donkey's harness and give his haunches a hardy slap.

Yosef stopped at the door, his own door, right where the centurion stood. They were only an arm's length away from each other. The carpenter wondered if the Roman might be able to kill him in a single stroke, even with the sword sheathed and his off-hand upon the hilt. Yosef placed the spear in front of him and rested it on the ground. Maybe it would block the first blow.

"Greetings, Yosef, son of Ya'akov," said Gaius. He spoke in the common Greek. His tone was civil.

"Greetings, Gaius," said Yosef. "Centurion. God-fearer. Giver." It was not the first time since he awoke that day that he regretted his inadequacy in Greek.

"Would you prefer to speak in Hebrew?" Gaius asked in near-perfect Hebrew. Only his accent betrayed him.

Before Yosef could respond, the foot-soldier roused himself from his drag-behind transport. It was an awkward set of motions, but he clamored out of his shield, kicking gear everywhere as he did so. He stumbled his way toward his commander.

The legionnaire's words were a thick tangle of Latin. Yosef did not understand a single word. But the tone and the message were unmistakable. Agonized though he was, murder dripped from every utterance.

While his intentions were clear, his manner was unbecoming. Yosef could see that much even on the centurion's expressionless face. Struggling to stand up at attention while also succumbing to the urge to double over, the foot-soldier looked like a drunkard caught desperately between the desire to finish a rousing story and the reflex to expel a festival's worth of drinking.

Gaius still didn't move. He listened to the report. The centurion received everything set before him with no indication of either assent or disinterest.

Once the legionnaire said all that he could, he folded over upon himself with his hands upon his knees another time. Yosef did not understand a single word, but he enjoyed the display of misery played out in the body of his son's assailant. It seemed as though the soldier was doing everything in his power not to place a hand over the member that suffered the most.

As if a child had just finished interrupting him at the dinner table, Gaius addressed Yosef once more. "Would you prefer that we spoke in Hebrew?" the centurion asked, once again in his impressive Hebrew. "I would not presume to use your Holy Language without your willingness."

"That would make things easier," Yosef inclined. "My Greek will only confuse the both of us."

"No," Gaius responded, "I don't think it can be any more confusing than the report that I was just given. It seems that you and your son attacked my soldier about a mile outside of town..? Seems an awfully strange thing to do, a carpenter and his young Torah-scholar."

As Yosef considered his response, the foot-soldier interrupted with another flurry of irate Latin. To the carpenter's undying surprise, the centurion back-handed the soldier with a closed fist, knocking him flat upon the ground. No sooner had the legionnaire collapsed than the centurion barked a single command. At that, the soldier stood up to his feet at attention, obviously managing several patches of pain. Blood ran from his lip as well as from another region not visible. With a stern look from his commander, the soldier remained frozen, awaiting orders, not daring another interruption.

"Please continue, Yosef," resumed the centurion. "Explain to me how you got the better of my soldier here, out there on the road, with nothing but your boy and your donkey and," Gaius looked behind Yosef, "and your baggage."

The father of the messiah was shocked beyond his senses, strained beyond his sensibilities. When the centurion struck the soldier, his left hand never departed from his sword-hilt. Was he nothing more than a sadist, saving one hand for each man, so as to strike one and slay the other?

The die had been cast. Yosef meant to catch it. He would tell the story exactly as it had occurred.

At first, Gaius remained impassive. When Yosef explained his broken Greek and the discourtesy of the ordeal, the centurion only nodded. Once the carpenter described the initial assault, Gaius's left hand gripped his hilt with a ferocious intention, but he did not unsheathe it. Yosef hesitated for a moment, but when the sword was not removed, he continued.

Then the father of the messiah detailed his rally with Shimshon. Gaius's face showed more than Yosef had ever seen before. His expression was a mix of incredulity, wonder and amusement.

"Show me," Gaius said.

"The donkey?" Yosef asked.

"Indeed," Gaius responded.

"A moment, sir," Yosef consented. "Permit me to unharness the creature and fetch him a snack."

Gaius nodded his agreement.

The carpenter leaned the spear against the wall of his home. With great care and deliberation, Yosef helped Yeshua dismount the donkey. Gaius observed as the boy's movements were stiff and stifled. In time, Shimmy was completely disburdened. Yeshua leaned against his father; Yosef held him close with one arm, supporting him as he embraced him.

Once Yosef had prepared Shimshon for his exhibition, he sounded the familiar whistles in their proper sequence. In spite of his long and heavy day, Shimshon was the good beast he had always been. He released one kick, then both kicks. Then he enjoyed his treat.

For the first time since their impromptu confrontation, Gaius removed his hand from his sword and folded both arms across his chest. He looked at the donkey, astounded. His gaze shifted to the soldier, who was struggling to remain upright.

After several moments of back-and-forth looking, his mind straining with the details, the centurion placed his right hand upon his mouth. Too many moments passed for Yosef's comfort, but there Gaius remained, one hand over his bald face while his eyes searched for truth. The carpenter kept himself and waited.

Abruptly, the centurion smacked the soldier in the belly. It wasn't much of a blow, barely enough to aggravate a man. But slapping right where a couple of donkey's hoofs had rapped just a few hours earlier was more than enough to drop the legionnaire to the ground yet again.

Once more, the centurion barked the same order in Latin. It was a more concerted effort the second go around, but the soldier groaned his way to standing at attention a second time. Stand as he might, he could not keep his face from its contortions.

Gaius looked at Yosef, bewildered. It had become Yosef's turn to remain impassive. The two men stood there staring at each other, both wondering what the other might say next. At long last, Gaius opened his mouth – and he laughed.

It was an eerie kind of laugh, the sound of a man encountering a side of the world he never thought to exist, much less to explore. The centurion was careless to both the hour as well as the neighbors. He approached Shimshon, howling uncontrollably and spurting out strange somethings in Latin, petting the donkey with congratulations and hilarity.

And then, forgetting himself, Gaius placed his hand on Yosef's shoulder, laughing freely, as if the two men had been in a tavern together all night.

"If only I could conscript you to train all of OUR donkeys!" the centurion bellowed.

Yosef gave a curt little grin in response, but he dared not laugh. He remained alert, suspicious. Amused as the commander seemed to be, the carpenter still had no inclination as to his standing during these proceedings. Several minutes went by as Gaius fawned over the donkey, still guffawing and intoning Latin affections. Eventually, the centurion collected himself and asked Yosef if that were all, to which Yosef responded gravely, "No."

Laughter left the commander entirely at the description of the rope-lashing and donkey-dragging. Hearing of the shed in the field, his face was sterner than it had been at any point thus far. His left hand returned to his sword hilt.

Yeshua had remained at Yosef's side ever since the kicking demonstration. Gaius studied him with that magisterial intensity, looking over the lad and surmising his purported abuses. Yeshua returned the man's gaze without flinching.

The young messiah had been dealt a heavy blow that day, enough to compromise his faculties and muster his excuses. But the boy had grit. Weak as his legs were and dizzy as his head was, he would not swoon or surrender so long as he could help it. Yosef had seen his son so help it many times before, enduring long hours past the point of fatigue in countless jobs during his apprenticeship. Nevertheless, the good carpenter wondered at the resolve of his child. Most boys his age would have asked to retreat into the house at the very onset of the incident. Not Yeshua. He was determined to remain by his Abba's side with all the strength that he could gather.

Then Yosef relayed the most audacious part of the hostilities. He had no idea what to expect by way of Gaius's reaction, but he portrayed the sequence of events with the same integrity of accuracy as he had displayed thus far. Yosef did not alter his tone or begin to appear apologetic. He relayed in Hebrew the difficulty he had during the interrogation in Greek, and he spared no detail of the soldier's threats in the retelling.

What the carpenter did with his knife to the legionnaire was unprecedented. While God-fearers had become a common enough occurrence culturally, the existence of circumcised Roman soldiers was an anomaly. That rite performed under duress was unheard of, save for a few isolated tales from times far ancient.

How everyone had returned was apparent as Gaius had witnessed their arrival. Yosef had no need to explain that. The construction of a makeshift stretcher and the arduous homecoming was of no interest after the details of the knifing.

"My plan did not include finding you at my doorstep tonight, Gaius," Yosef said.

There wasn't much room for surprise after the display of a combative donkey. Yet, Gaius found himself surprised again. The evil intention of the soldier was not so shocking, even though the centurion loathed it. He was familiar with the pederasty of the Romans, whether infantry or nobility. But he despised the practice. Nevertheless, he was a commander in the Roman army. Certain customs, no matter how heinous, were systemic.

However, the temerarious boldness of the carpenter was something else altogether. There were uprisings, rebellions and vandalisms that the Romans expected. But this? It didn't make any sense.

"Show me," said Gaius in Greek, as he turned his face toward the soldier.

Already pale in the face, the soldier blanched all the more. He remained frozen at attention except for the painful trembling in his body. He did not know what to show his commander... or he did not want to know.

Yosef looked on as the two of them exchanged a couple of sentences in Latin. Gaius was insistent. The soldier was horrified and motionless.

Then Gaius made a sudden open-handed swat at the soldier's nether region. The swiftness with which the man moved was frightening. This had become the third time that Yosef saw the centurion go from complete, dignified rest into an instantaneous, ferocious assault with no forewarning. How he commanded his body was a marvel in itself, but how he governed his face from his thoughts was even more baffling. What kind of man was this that would switch from civil discourse to violent determination, and back again, with no indication of discomfiture or frustration?

That swat never landed; Gaius hardly flicked the man's tunic. But the mere proximity of a most savage hand about his most sensitive hidden-away dropped the soldier to the ground all the same. Flinching in anticipation of the smack was enough to throw him into his familiar agony in the dirt. The legionnaire writhed as if he had been cut once again.

Beholding the sight, Gaius turned to Yosef with a face gone wild. The carpenter thought that he saw murder in the man's eyes. For all Yosef knew, he might find himself on the receiving end of one of those unannounced and unpredictable attacks from the dangerous commander. He considered the distance of a desperate lunge to the spear, the sword at his waist, the presence of Yeshua still cradled in his arm; he remembered how deft and deadly were every single one of the centurion's movements. Yosef's prospects were slim if not futile.

Gaius howled again, louder and longer than the first time. If he had laughed like a maniac after Shimshon's display, then he sounded like a madman's nightmare upon the evidence of circumcision. And the wildness never left his hysteria.

The man became a storm of movement. His composure vanished into the night; his habit of stateliness had been overtaken by the preposterous ordeal that had been presented to him. As a commander of soldiers given to drunkenness, debauchery and all manner of foolhardy escapades, Gaius had lost his capacity for surprise after only a few years in his position. However, this was something else. He had no notion of what to do with the report, whether to involve his superiors. He knew even less what to do with the problem of one of his soldiers wounded at the hands of a Jew.

Yet, somehow, he was free for a spell. Gaius found himself in a euphoria the likes of which he had only experienced in the triumph of battle or in the throes of passion. This was not the night that he had been expecting. He had been pensive and aggravated standing in waiting at Yosef's stoop for hours on end. But this had become a perfect moment in time.

Minutes beyond counting passed in the centurion's fit. He recollected himself, wiping tears from his face and clearing away the aftershock chuckles that would vie for his attention. In that serenity, he found his presence of mind once again. Whatever the risks might entail, the way had become clear to him.

Yosef and Yeshua never had any inclination to be at ease. While the centurion had been heedless, father and son remained resolute. The Romans were dangerous occupiers. Many Jews had been lulled into false confidences and illusions of security. Yosef's family, his colleagues in the synagogue, the whole of the Pharisaic party – they would not compromise their faithfulness and ally themselves with the Romans like the Sadducees or the Herodians had done. That was the rule during even the most innocuous of interactions with the Gentiles. This moment was much more perilous. No amount of laughter could have softened their memory or swayed their perseverance.

Gaius must have surmised as much. He was an unusual Roman, after all, benefactor to their synagogue and truehearted God-fearer. But Yosef had no way of inferring his intentions, especially not when his devotion to the Empire was pitted against his fascination with the God of Yisrael.

"What are we going to do, Yosef?" Gaius asked.

"Is there a way for us to make peace?" Yosef returned.

The two men looked at each other for an age. Neither of them flinched. No one stirred, save the soldier who had remained in his hump of hurt in the dirt.

Then Gaius addressed the soldier in Latin once more. Surprisingly, he spoke to him more softly than he had at any other point thus far. Only a few sentences passed in that communication. At the end of it, the legionnaire stood up and faced Yosef and Yeshua.

"I am sorry for the evil that I have done to you," he said in Greek, "and for the evil that I would have done to you."

"I forgive," Yosef said. "Peace."

"Peace," the soldier responded. He stole a glance at his commander.

Just as everything seemed like all would be right in their fractured world, Yeshua left his father's side and approached the soldier, who was then standing next to the centurion. Yosef's eyes widened in terror. They had spoken peace to each other! What was the boy thinking?

The two Romans glanced at each other for an instant as they looked at the lad standing in front of them, holding their attention in his grasp. Yeshua looked to his right at the centurion, then directly at the soldier before him. And the boy had the audacity to point straight at the man's injury.

"What you have lost tonight is nothing compared to how much more you have yet to lose," Yeshua warned. He spoke in a Greek that was equal in quality to the centurion's Hebrew.

Yosef was aghast at what his son had just uttered. He was also surprised at Yeshua's proficiency in Greek. He knew that his son was studious, but he had no idea that he had already become that accomplished. As he found himself doing so many times a week, no matter the setting, the father of the messiah looked at his son with newfound wonder. Nevertheless, he was gobsmacked by the menacing tone that followed their declaration of peace.

Gaius was disconcerted, too. He also noted the father's surprise over his son. Not much left the commander's observation.

Despite his day, the soldier actually had the steam to get angry. He didn't speak, but he glowered at the little Jew taunting him in his injury, threatening him of future hurts. His eyes stole left toward his commander as if he wondered at his allowances before such words.

"Your life, soldier, your soul, is of great value," Yeshua said. "But you would make it worthless if you continue to waste your days away in evil."

All three of the men looked up at each other in surprise. The Romans thought that Yosef might interject. He did not. The father of the messiah was as unsure as the two of them.

"The God of Yisrael would smile upon you, child. Seek Him out. Be at peace. Go – and sin no more." Yeshua spoke into the darkness of that night and vanquished the confusion of their hearts.

Silence hovered over the four men for time beyond reckoning. There was nothing more to say. No one wanted to say anything.

Eventually, Gaius broke the quiet and addressed the soldier in Latin one last time. The legionnaire bowed before the two Jews with impressive grace. As he straightened up, he looked long upon Yeshua, with a curious array of emotions on his face. Then he gathered his effects, did an about-face, and limped toward the garrison.

Once the soldier had departed, Gaius addressed Yeshua directly.

"Thank you for your words, young master. I imagine you have many hurts awaiting your mother's care. Certainly, she is eager to see you as well. Would you mind if I spoke with your father for a moment?"

"Thank you for your patience and good judgment, commander," Yeshua responded. "May the God of Peace grant you the Truth that you seek."

"Amen," Gaius said, in Hebrew.

"Amen," replied Yosef and Yeshua.

Yeshua looked at Yosef for reassurance. The good carpenter nodded. The young lad turned toward the door.

"Young master!" Gaius called out to Yeshua just before he knocked upon the door for entry.

"Yes, commander," Yeshua replied, looking back.

"I hope that one day my son and yourself might have the opportunity to become friends," Gaius said.

Such friendships between Romans and Jews were not to be had, not even within the context of God-fearers inside a synagogue. All three of them standing there knew as much. The centurion was sincere in what he said, but they all understood that, in the end, it was a polite and sentimental nothing to wish out loud.

"What is his name?" Yeshua asked.

"Cornelius," the centurion smiled.

"I will remember him," Yeshua smiled in return. "I will begin praying for him this very night."

The centurion could see the full force of Yeshua's sincerity. The remembrance and prayers promised were as gifts that Gaius could handle. What the young master had spoken was far from a polite and sentimental nothing. The Roman felt his world more complete in the assurance that had been given to him.

Yeshua rapped his signature knock on the door. The scurry of work to open the door from the inside began right away. Miriam had been waiting there all along. Yeshua was inside the house within moments. All manner of commotion came to life within the house. Many bodies were evidently engaged. The door closed a moment later.

At last, only the carpenter and the centurion remained outside, along with the victorious donkey idling patiently behind them. They looked upon each other like they would after their times in the synagogue on Shabbat. The gaze was the same, but the passage of that day had changed everything. And yet, their worlds had become no different. The divide of two cultures imposed by an Empire would not be erased in a single night, perhaps not even in a lifetime. Nevertheless, they saw each other anew. Something had changed in spite of themselves, in spite of the hostilities into which they had both been born.

"You know, Yosef," Gaius began, "we Romans like to joke that when you Jews cut off the foreskin on each other, you must end up cutting off much more!"

"Well," Yosef retorted, "we Jews don't bother ourselves about the condition of Roman organs."

Gaius laughed at that. "Well met, good sir! Well met. Nevertheless, I have to tell you. After everything that I have seen and heard tonight, I would stake the whole of my career on the gamble that you have, what shall I say... spheres... to make even Romulus and Remus envious!"

The centurion clapped Yosef on the shoulder as if they were colleagues. To which Yosef only looked back at the man stunned. What would he do with this conviviality?

Gaius thought that perhaps his Hebrew had been imprecise. So, he repeated himself, the next time pantomiming with his hands below his waist as to what region he was complimenting. Yosef was unmoved by the compliment and the gestures.

"Oh, come now, Yosef!" Gaius demanded. "Do you Jews place no value on the size of a man's sire-standard?"

Yosef finally allowed himself a curt smile as he responded, "We Jews measure more about manhood than one member. But thank you. You are an impressive man yourself, Gaius. Truly, I am grateful. This was a terrible day. After I had made my stroke, I did not know how things would turn out. I did not expect to see you tonight, not yet. Nevertheless, I must ask. Will this be the end of the matter?"

Gaius placed one hand on his bare chin. "I don't expect anything else to develop. Your plan was crazy, but it is strangely efficient. He will be too ashamed to tell anyone else of the ordeal. He knows that I know. He wouldn't dare cross me. Long-term... I suppose I have a few days to work out the details of his fate, isn't that right?"

"Oh," Yosef raised his eyebrows, "if he has any duty in the next three days, they will be the worst in his life."

The centurion stifled a chortle. "I'll see about that. No, I'll tell you true, Yosef, that one's pederasty is beyond the bounds even of Roman allowances. He has caused a great deal of strife in our garrison, crossing the lines between other men and their boys. I despise the practice. Your people have taught me a great deal, Yosef. I hope you realize how much I esteem the wisdom of your Torah... and how much I hope that your God..."

Gaius stopped himself. He looked around, as if someone else might hear them. Even after seeing that they were still very much alone, the centurion said no more. He simply looked at Yosef with something like a plea in his eyes, the antithesis of a face that a centurion should wear.

The good carpenter saw the desperation and felt pity, or mercy... compassion perhaps. Yosef didn't know what to call it. But he felt it. And he determined to give it to the man, enemy of his people or not.

"I understand, commander," Yosef said. "As my son said, I pray that you would find peace. Perhaps we will not see happy days in this world, when our sons would study together and our wives would become as sisters. Much strife remains between our peoples. But..."

Then Yosef stopped himself. It was his turn to look around. He knew that they were alone. But could he trust himself with the words that were screaming in his heart? He didn't know. He fidgeted at the bare spot of skin inside his beard for a moment.

This had already been an immeasurable day and an unreal night of firsts. Might as well risk another gamble, Yosef mused.

The father of the messiah took a deep breath and reached out his hand toward the centurion. The two men clasped hands as if it were an embrace. They looked each other full in the face.

"If I should find you in the World to Come, Gaius," Yosef declared, "then I would gladly welcome you as my neighbor."

Both men, carpenter and centurion, welled up before each other. Neither of them knew the rules of their respective cultures, and they did not want to disgrace one another. They heartily gripped one another's hands and gave each other a good jostling. Then they cleared their throats and bid each other a good night. Both of them meant to protect the other's dignity.

Gaius good-nighted Yosef once more as he turned away in a brisk pace and headed toward the garrison. Yosef stood there musing for a time, watching the centurion all the way up the street. That moment would be with him in secret for the rest of his life. He would never tell anyone else what they had spoken.

At last, Yosef recollected himself. As delicately as he could, he put Shimshon to bed for the night. Their donkey had saved the day no less than twice, perhaps more that the carpenter had not yet realized.

With his creature tended, the street of stony steps quiet again, the carpenter was overdue to take to his own care. He looked around one last time. Yosef was home and he was long overdue to go inside.

11

Legacy, Conspiracy, Sufficiency

MIRIAM CAPTURED YOSEF in her embrace like the wife who had been waiting for her husband to return from war. The carpenter felt many of his aches amplified within her clutches, but those pains drowned within the enveloping sweetness of her affections. His mind was swimming inside of the raging waters of the day's events, many of which he did not think that he could bring himself to divulge to his wife. However, the mere presence of Miriam brought a stillness to the turbulence of Yosef's soul. She could hurt him all that she wanted. This was the best discomfort that Yosef had felt all that long day.

"You smell like blood," Miriam stated. She was teasing him, but Yosef could hear her concern in the slightest hint of tears behind her voice.

"You should smell the other man," Yosef rejoined, "but that would be inappropriate."

The mother of the messiah squeezed the humor out of her husband so that he finally laughed in his discomfort. She did not relent. Miriam had her man back to herself and she was not keen on letting him go.

Elisheva, Zechariya and Yochanan waited patiently as husband and wife received one another. Concern and relief wore on their faces in equal measure. With no more Roman cadre at the door, all anxieties were rapidly falling away.

"Do we have any wine, Beloved?" Yosef asked. "I would like to sit down with the family for a time before we all become weary again."

Yosef had no strong desire to break away from the embrace. He did, however, very much want to clean himself at least somewhat before lingering with his woman any longer. The blood from his wound had been dried to his body for several hours. A change of clothes and a discreet rinse was in order. Having asked his wife to prepare something to drink insured that she would not bear witness to stains that looked worse than they were.

"I'll see what we can work up," Miriam responded. She held him close for another few moments before releasing him from her domain. It had been a long day for her as well.

The good carpenter greeted their family that had been standing by so graciously. Elisheva, Zechariya and Yochanan each hugged Yosef briefly in turn. They had heard the exchange with Miriam and understood that he would return to them soon.

Miriam and Elisheva began preparing a mulled wine while Zechariya and Yochanan proceeded to set the table. Yosef looked at his family members busying themselves in the kitchen and dining room, taking a moment to appreciate something as mundane as table-setting and beverage-making. It was a welcome sight to follow the other things he had been forced to see.

Before going to his bedroom, he looked into the children's room, stealing in as quietly as he could. Yeshua was not there. Yosef guessed that he must have gone to the privy.

Virtually every night of his life, Yosef went into their quarters as they slept. The tenor of his little ones breathing softly in the safety of their beds was his favorite sound in all Creation. He would touch each of them lightly, not wanting to wake them, but needing to make his prayers for them something physical, hoping to pass his blessing onto them even as they dreamed. After a most harrowing day, he listened as if he had never heard their night-song before. This ritual was always meaningful, but that night it was sacred, necessary, healing.

Having found all of his people safe and sound and secure and just like normal, Yosef went to his room and tended to himself. Changing and washing after a tradesman's day was its own deliberation. Going through the same motions after a battle, brief as it was, was another thing entirely. Everything hurt. His whole body was stiff with all of the aches: narrowly escaping death, almost losing his son, striking his knife against a pagan, the hefting, the hiking, the scheming and hoping, not to mention the many heart-hurts.

He placed his tefillin and tallit within their cases and reminded himself about the repair that his head tefilla required. Removing the tefilla from his head was as arduous as it was delicate. Bringing water to the wound at the back of his skull was an excruciating scald of lights in his vision. His hair was matted with blood. He would be in for a painful bath in the morning.

With a fresh change of clothes and a somewhat refreshed body, Yosef was prepared to greet his family more fully. He found them seated at the table, each of them with a full cup in their hands and a full pitcher before them. Yosef welled up simply at the sight of his family and the familiar stoneware of their table. The father of the messiah smiled at everyone. He was unspeakably glad to have them. Zechariya stood up and handed the carpenter his favorite vessel, filled to the brim with mulled wine.

It was warm to the hands, to the nose and to the palate. Yosef enjoyed wine in all its forms, but Miriam intuited the perfect thing for him on that night. A subtle addition of their favorite spices was added to the concoction with pomegranate seeds thrown into the brew for its tangy sweetness. A sliced pomegranate was left on the table for anyone wishing to add more to their drink. Miriam had also arranged almonds, dates, figs and matzah for everyone.

They did not usually indulge in such an opulent spread during the week, but it had been quite the night. It was good for everyone to enjoy a bit of frivolous nourishment. To occupy themselves with food and drink and one another's company would begin to put some distance between their shared togetherness and the ordeal behind them. The Jews had learned to practice clinging to joy in those fleeting moments between the last hardship and the next trial. In the years of the Roman occupation, that punctuation was perpetual.

Yosef sat down at the head of the table and only then realized that the person seated to his right was Yeshua. He looked well, which was a gift to behold. Still, the good carpenter wondered how much his son was simply putting a good face in front of his hidden afflictions.

"I had thought that you might welcome a fast and sudden sleep, Yeshua!" Yosef inquired.

"Not as much as I would welcome your words, Abba," Yeshua replied. "You said that you wanted to talk."

"What are you trying to do to the boy?" Miriam demanded. "After the day that he's had?" She was sitting to Yosef's left so that he suddenly felt trapped between an accidental accuser and a zealous inquisitor.

"Well, I didn't say that I had to talk to him tonight, Miriam!" Yosef flustered. "All that I have been trying to do today is get him home!"

"Then what is he talking about?" Miriam returned.

"He's talking about a talk that we can have another time!" Yosef insisted. "Can a man enjoy his wine and his in-laws for a few moments before he commits to a new argument with his wife?"

Yosef and Miriam stared at each other in silence, each of them calculating how much further they would get embroiled in the developing hostility. Neither of them intended their tones. It was very unlike them to argue so hastily, without much restraint. However, they had both been tested that day to extremes for which no one ever prepares. Tempers that they had kept in check with their enemies were beginning to spill out upon each other. It was a sad irony, but their love for each other established the kind of safety in which they could at times hurt each other without wanting to.

"My loves," Elisheva interrupted their intense gaze and beheld them with her penetrating gray eyes.

"I think that you are both exhausted after longing for each other all day. Would you like for us to leave the two of you alone for the night?"

Elisheva's question was sincere. Yet her insinuation was cunning. Without rebuking them to the point of humiliation, she managed to usher in a hush to remind them of their deeper feelings and their truest selves.

Yosef and Miriam softened as they looked at each other anew. They clasped hands and gave one another an understanding nod. The rest of the table understood as well. Husband and wife would have much to discuss later, but they had reestablished the peace of the home.

"Son," said Yosef, "I never meant that we had to talk right away tonight. You've had a hard day. We can speak later. Truly, that wouldn't bother me at all. Would you like to be done and lay yourself down for the night?"

"Thank you, Abba," Yeshua replied, "but I'm fine to have our discussion now. I think it's best that we talk about it finally. And it's appropriate that Ima's family is here with us, too."

"What do you mean?" Yosef faltered for a moment. "I only meant to have a talk with you, Yeshua. I never meant to involve everyone while they're visiting us."

"Well, don't you think it's appropriate, Abba?" Yeshua returned.

At that, Yosef realized that Yeshua knew what the conversation would be about. He shouldn't have been surprised, the carpenter realized, but he was all the same. That was the sensation with this boy – each and every time. How could the boy know? Yet, after all his years, how could Yosef not anticipate his son's prescience?

"Yeshua, how..?" Yosef asked. He could not help himself from asking, neither could he complete his question.

"I'm thirteen, Abba," Yeshua replied. He did not interrupt his father so much as he came alongside his thoughts. "You are concerned with my maturation, as all fathers are. And because of the prophecies that you and Ima have carried, you are worried about my kingship, that I am not being prepared. I know that you've been trying to talk to me about this for months. But we've had so many other things to talk about that you have given me space at every turn. After the violence that we suffered today, the urgency is upon you more than ever before. You have been a good, good Abba to me. I will be a good son to you tonight. Let us see this burden removed from your strong shoulders."

Yosef was stumped. His son had done more than deduce his thoughts. Yosef felt as though Yeshua looked into the most tucked away prayers of his heart and read them there. The boy had a way of rendering the difficult deliberations as times of tenderness.

Precious as the moment was, it was the last accumulation of emotional weight that Yosef could endure. He had kept himself together through everything else that day. From the slow start that morning to the public humiliation before the Roman soldier, the forced march and the vicious assault, his fear over his son and his fury before the legionnaire, the desperate scheme and the grim trudge back, all the way to the culmination of the reckoning with Gaius – Yosef had kept himself composed through it all, his emotions checked by his discipline and his wits, albeit having a brief dispute with Miriam.

Even there in the safety of his own home, in the comfort of the people he loved best, the father of the messiah tried his hardest to quell the storm that was looming over his entire soul. Nevertheless, he was finally undone. His people had gotten the better of him. His resilience no longer had any purpose.

Yosef wept.

In the instant that the man began to break, Yeshua got out of his seat and went to his Abba. Yeshua stepped forward to embrace his father, to which Yosef reached out and grabbed a hold of his son like a man clinging to the surface of a capsized boat. The carpenter buried his face in his son's chest and he wailed.

It was a lament that spanned years of his spirit, kept locked away in the recesses of his secrets lest the grief debilitate him. His guts sank at the memory of Miriam's pregnancy fourteen years prior; his legs quaked at the vision of their escape from Herod; his heart tremored at the reminder of shared loneliness with the exiled Jews in Alexandria; his palms sweated when he recalled frantically looking for Yeshua in Yerushalayim; his chest heaved at the bodily terror of their many narrow escapes that very day. Yosef cried for everything.

The good carpenter cried about not being the blood-father of this boy he loved like his own. He sobbed at the murmur of guilt for not deserving to steward a child so noble as this one. He keened about the fear of failing the high calling upon his life. Yosef bawled and whimpered and moaned.

He felt Miriam standing behind his chair, leaning on his back, wrapping her arms around both of her boys. Elisheva and Zechariya came to his side and placed their hands on him, embracing him as they could. Yochanan stood nearby a little awkward although sincere. They remained with him until he was free of all of it.

As monstrous as the thunder was that overtook him, so was the breeze of levity that blew through the room in his newfound liberation. His body had borne many hurts, the physical injuries being the least part of the toll. The excavation of the wounds of memory was beyond Yosef's ken and frame to bear, beyond his capacity for speech or understanding. That song of tears ran through his entire person and carried away the detritus that had amassed in his being. In the caring arms of his family that had come alongside of him in his release, Yosef became lighter than he had been in years. The load had been lifted, heavier and longer borne than he could have known. He became free.

Zechariya prayed over his friend briefly. He thanked God for strength, healing and joy. He was a good priest and knew better than to overly formalize the prayer and ruin the peace.

"Blessed are You, Adonai, our God, King of the Universe, Who has kept us alive, sustained us, and brought us forth to this season."

Yosef looked up with his wet face and chuckled, just a little, as he croaked, "may I have a rag?"

His family giggled with him as a rag was fetched. They were glad to see him whole. The burden that had fallen away from him brightened the whole room as it lightened his frame.

He wiped his face and his beard and then blew his nose. Everyone returned to their seats. Yosef picked up his cup of wine and took a deep draft down to his core.

"Good talk, everybody," Yosef quipped as he set down his vessel.

The clan laughed freely. Their man was restored. They enjoyed the privilege of attending to his need.

"Our son wants to talk, Yosef," Miriam said, "so why don't you let him talk?"

Yosef looked at his wife to find her smirking at him. She was teasing him as well as making light of her own earlier conduct. He liked it.

"Are you sure that you want to do this with your cousin, your aunt and your uncle here, son?" Yosef asked.

Yeshua was looking at his parents over the rim of his cup, his forearms leaning against the table.

"They belong here for this, Abba," Yeshua replied and set his vessel down. "We are the only people in the world that know what's before us. The six of us are the insurgence. These are plans that we should make together."

The good carpenter looked to his in-laws. Despite the ordeal of the day and the most sudden paroxysm they had witnessed, their faces were enthusiastic. They showed no signs of weariness. The light of Jewish fervor shined bright on their faces.

"All right," Yosef said. "Where should we begin?"

"What are your concerns?" Yeshua returned.

"Well, do you think that you are ready to become king, Yeshua?" Yosef responded.

"Aside from age and anointing," Yeshua rejoined, "what do I lack?"

"Do you have any military training? Or understanding of economics? Have you developed a plan to overtake the Romans and restore our Land? Who will teach you these things?" Yosef probed.

"Is it power and wealth that Yisrael needs most?" Yeshua challenged.

"How else are we going to defeat the occupiers?" Yochanan interrupted. He was brash, but not impertinent. There was just the slightest shade of a shift in the cousins' relationship ever since their scrap at the river.

"I tell you true, Yani," Yeshua replied, "neither swords nor gold will avail us of the Romans."

"Then what is your strategy, young messiah?" Zechariya asked. Everyone straightened up at the designation, save for Yeshua himself. They all knew what they were talking about, but the title brought a hue of potency to the conversation that had to that point only been implied. Stating it plainly, the priest brought a specificity to the conversation that quickened their perspective and jolted their attention.

"My calling, Uncle" Yeshua stated, "is to seek and to save the lost sheep of Yisrael."

"How can you save them without delivering them from the invaders?" Miriam asked.

"Yes, son," Yosef reiterated, "what is salvation without deliverance?"

Yeshua looked at each one of them in turn, from his cousin, to his aunt and uncle, to his parents. His wine-dark eyes beheld them such that they could not turn away from his gaze. In that stillness, Yeshua made the table his own.

He plucked a few seeds from the open pomegranate at the center of the table and crushed them between his fingers one at a time, releasing the juice from within. With the middle finger of his right hand, he began doodling on the table, drawing strange lines with the fruit's liquid. Everyone else glanced at each other as they waited for him to respond.

"Did King David have any training before he battled Golyat?" Yeshua posed. "Or Gid'on before him? How about our father Avraham ages before that? Each of these men did battle victoriously without having been trained how to do so. And you would have me muster my troops and rally my commanders even now?"

No one answered.

"'Five of you will chase one hundred and one hundred of you will chase ten thousand,'" Yeshua recited. "No, it is not military might that is the problem that besets us. Neither is it wealth. 'If only you would carefully listen to the voice of Adonai your God, being careful to do all these mitzvot that I am commanding you today! For Adonai your God will bless you as He promised you. So, you will lend to many nations, but not borrow; you will rule over many nations, but they will not rule over you.' You see, Adonai does not need our currency to buy us back for Himself."

Yeshua paused to look at everyone once again. "What Yisrael finds wanting is obedience. The blessings and the curses of HaShem, blessed is He, have never changed. Whenever his children have kept Torah, they have lived in bounty; when they have strayed from His ways, He has stricken them. The only deliverance Yisrael requires is from its own waywardness."

His family was alarmed. Their young man had come of age but he was not yet full-grown and there he was declaring the fates of nations as though they were his to portend. What's more, he did not vilify the Romans for the plight of his people. Instead, he had the gall to lay their oppression at their own feet.

"Yeshua," Zechariya began, "have our people not been faithful since the days of Zerubbabel, Ezra and Nechemyah? In their exile, they cried out to Adonai in repentance and sought His face. They learned Torah so that they could do Torah so that they could teach Torah. And the Temple was rebuilt! And the men of the Great Assembly endure to this day! So it is that we today, all of us, learn and do and teach Torah. All Yisrael keeps the Shabbat and the mitzvot! If our people were still errant, then how could HaShem, blessed is He, send us His messiah at such a time as this? What more of the Torah do we lack in our keeping?"

The good priest spoke true. He gave voice to the thoughts of the others present. There was vitality in the history that he portrayed. They all knew it well.

Yeshua continued scrawling his strange portrait of pomegranate juice. "Uncle, the men of the Great Assembly recaptured everything of the Torah, except for its essence."

They all gaped at his uncanny boldness. A thirteen-year-old boy did not just casually call into question the authority of the Sanhedrin. What was he thinking to assert that the essence of Torah was lost on them?

"What is the essence of Torah?" Yeshua asked.

"'That which is hateful to you, do not do to your neighbor,'" Yochanan replied. "Hillel taught us that."

"Amen, cousin," Yeshua agreed. "'And you shall love your neighbor as yourself.' Now, tell me, have the children of Yisrael learned how to love their neighbors?"

Once again, they only looked at him with unease.

"Perhaps you would say to me that we do love our neighbor," Yeshua resumed. "And I would ask you about the Samaritans. Even now, you detest the mere mention of them. For, you say, they have not been faithful to Torah. True enough, they have not yet learned to submit to all of His instruction. However, the children of Yisrael deny the Samaritans the same grace that has been poured over themselves throughout all of the story of the Scriptures. How many times has HaShem forgiven His children and restored them to their Land? And we would refuse to bear with the Samaritans in their tutelage for a time?

"Then, perhaps you would refuse the Samaritans regardless, not being children of the covenant. You would tell me that the Jews love their brethren, their real neighbors. And I would show you the hatred between Essene and Herodian, between Pharisee and Sadducee. Even their fellow Jews they hold in contempt.

"Of course, you would tell me that Sadducees are not worthy of love, since they are given to heresy and corruption. To which I would show you the Pharisees and their jostling for position, their obsession with obeisance and hierarchy. They pride themselves on their keeping of Torah. Yet they have not valued above all the love for their neighbor.

"I tell you true: the essence of the Torah is Love. And love is never more fully demonstrated than in forgiveness. Until we have learned to love even our enemies, we shall not prevail. Yisrael shall never defeat Rome without first becoming a land where forgiveness flows like rivers of wine. Then all the nations would come to us for the waters of mikveh.

"Yisrael wants for a king, but her children need for a teacher."

It was an astounding condensation. Yeshua spoke in a manner unlike any of the sages. Even as the presentation was upsetting, the family at the table reeled at the density of one idea strung to the next. There was nothing to refute, yet the unease remained.

"How will you teach them to love all of their neighbors, Yeshua?" Elisheva asked. "What will you do that the Prophets have not already done?"

"I will give myself to them, Auntie," said Yeshua. "I will teach them by placing my love ever before them. I will fill the Torah full of meaning in their ears. In time, they will come to know the Truth."

"What if I'm right, son" Yosef determined, "even just a little bit right?"

"About my kingship?" Yeshua asked.

"After what happened today," Yosef hesitated, "I must insist that you learn something of warfare. That... what happened... that cannot happen again..."

Yeshua placed his hand over Yosef's. "Where would I learn what you require of me, Abba?"

"Well," Yosef stole a glance to Miriam, cleared his throat, and stated, "I know of a man. He is one of the Zealot leaders. I have spoken to him about you before."

"You want our son to join one of the rebellions?" Miriam demanded.

Yosef sighed. "No... at least not yet... I don't know exactly! All I know is that David didn't stand before Golyat without weapons as well as knowledge in his hands of what to do with them! Our son has nothing of the sort. Are we really going to send him out of the house, to attain his kingship, with no training of any kind?"

"What is a bandit going to teach our son, Yosef?" Miriam responded.

"Miriam, this man and many others like him are training up young men all over the Land," Yosef explained. "Yeshua won't become part of a revolt, at least not for a time. They are planning a great uprising, years from now. So, they are teaching the skills of battle to all the young men that they can gather. When the time is right, they will have an army spread all over the country, ready to respond in force from our secrets scattered all across the sands."

The mother of the messiah knitted her brow and crossed her arms. Yosef recognized the posture. Miriam assumed that demeanor whenever she had nothing more to say but had not yet come around to liking the matter. It was a small concession. The good carpenter would give her space to reckon with things on her own terms, in her own time.

"I do not think that the sword will be of use in my ministry, Abba," Yeshua said.

"Do you think that you could not learn anything of value from such a fellow, son?" Yosef inquired.

Yeshua considered that for a moment as he continued to dally with his dribble scribble on the table. "Perhaps... do you think he knows anything about hiding?"

"They are subversive agitators, Yeshua," Yosef responded. "Hiding is the greatest part of their fighting."

With two quick flourishes, Yeshua appeared to finish his drawing. He reached for a rag on the table and wiped his finger dry. He looked at what he had streaked and seemed satisfied with himself.

"I am submitted to you, Abba," Yeshua conceded. "I will go where you instruct me to go. Tomorrow then?"

His family couldn't believe it. This boy, whom they had thought was intractable in his position had spun himself on a shekel in the other direction. Not to mention that he had yet to sleep since his attack. Was he serious?

"Why don't we all go to bed for the night," Miriam suggested. "We can resume this conversation in the morning. Agreed?"

Everyone readily assented, Yeshua and Yosef alike. They all finished their remaining sips of wine, bid each other good night, and went off to their respective beds. Only Yosef remained sitting at the table.

"Shall I see you shortly, my Beloved?" Miriam asked.

"Indeed, Beloved," Yosef promised, "I'll only be a moment."

They kissed one another's hands and Miriam departed.

All alone at the table, Yosef poured himself another cup of wine from the pitcher, emptying its contents. It was no longer warm, but it still satisfied. For the first time since he woke up, Yosef was by himself. A spell to see his own mind would put him in a better frame to lie down.

His thoughts skipped across all of the happenings. It was among the most eventful passages of the sun that he had ever experienced. Many of the thoughts he left behind as quickly as he remembered them. Others he let linger for a time. The wine would taste differently along with his reflections.

The father of the messiah let his eyes drift to where Yeshua had doodled with the pomegranate juice. Yosef stood up to look at it better, the dim oil lamp at the table being shy with its light. Looking down at what his son had drawn, it no longer looked messy. Immediately, he saw the outline of their nation, the Land of Yisrael.

Although, there was another set of lines beyond those borders that did not make sense to the carpenter. He wondered whether Yeshua had simply tried to spread out the juice so that it wasn't blotched in one place. But no. He had left pools for the Salt Sea and the Sea of Kinneret; slender streaks ran long throughout as the river courses. These weren't wasted lines on the outside of Yeshua's little map. Yosef could observe the same care of cartography in their movements as in the rest of the sketch.

Then Yosef saw it. Yeshua had drawn the Land of Yisrael as it was, and beyond that he had drawn the extended boundary markers of the most ancient prophecies. No king or judge had ever conquered those territories. Yet, the children of Yisrael remembered her promises. They believed that the messiah would deliver those lands in the days of his kingship.

While they had been debating and discussing, while Yeshua was stringing the pearls of Torah before their eyes, he was also casually gliding his finger upon the table into the shape of the Land to which he had been born as well as the outermost reaches of the realm in its future fullness. Yosef did not understand what his son meant about becoming a teacher rather than a king. And he still had his suspicions about the urgency of military readiness. However, looking at the elegant map set before him, the father of the messiah had to admit the incredible truth to himself.

Yeshua knew all about the Kingdom.

12

The First Encounter

YOSEF WOKE UP to a day-bright sun bursting upon every hand-breadth of his bedroom. He knew right away that he had overslept dreadfully late. The shock of embarrassment jolted him straight out of bed. He felt like he would be chasing the rest of the day like a Roman messenger leaning all the way into the gait of his sprint.

He slowed himself down just enough to pray the Shema. Then he donned his tefillin and tallit in reverence, albeit in a hurry. Yosef was flustered as he stepped outside his bedroom door.

His household was in a flurry of motion, his littlest children scurrying past him with hugs and "good morning, Abba" each in their turns. Miriam was in the kitchen preparing what she had saved for him that breakfast. Zechariya and Elisheva sat at the table.

"Good morning, Yosef," Zechariya greeted.

"Good morning, old friend," replied Yosef. "I'm sorry for my manner this morning."

"Tsk," chided Elisheva. "Say nothing of it. After your adventure yesterday? We thought that we might not see you until past noon."

Miriam placed his breakfast before him where he sat and leaned down to kiss his forehead.

"How do you feel, my Love?" she asked.

The good carpenter had not considered that question until his wife had asked him. Seeing his family at ease about the hour, hearing the sound of his people in happy activity inside and outside of the house, the three little ones scampering on the rooftop, he allowed himself to slow down and turn inward. Heeding his body, he felt stiff and sore in many places, a feeling that he would have for a week or so, more likely than not. However, beneath that, he realized that he had slept deep and full. He was rejuvenated. In spite of his aches and the many tears shed the night before, the relief of finally having the big talk with Yeshua allowed Yosef to breath more freely than he had since time beyond memory. The body could not know the weight of its baggage, the many burdens carried for so long that they coalesced with the courier, until the load had finally been laid down. Yosef was discovering his agility of soul and nimbleness of mind even as he considered his disburdenment.

"I feel great," Yosef answered. He meant it. What pains he bore from the day before were minuscule in comparison to the newfound exhilaration that he was breathing in.

Miriam kissed him again and hugged his neck. She left him with his breakfast and sat next to Elisheva at the table. The two ladies resumed their conversation with Zechariya as Yosef was given the space to himself to wake up fully to the day. All four of them sat at the same table, but there was an unspoken understanding that the good carpenter would be neither a host nor a participant right away.

Having the time to himself, Yosef meditated on the parashah of that week as he ate.

"The secret things belong to Adonai our God, but the things revealed belong to us and to our children forever – in order to do all the words of this Torah."

Yosef turned that passage over within his mind, as though it were a jewel held up to the light. He wanted to count how many truths refracted from a single question's diffuse penetration, how many angles of wisdom were available on its multifaceted surface, what depths remained that he might peer into for a lifetime. Yosef had not been turning the diamond for very long before a proverb came vying for his attention.

"It is the glory of God to conceal a matter
and the glory of kings to search it out."

There was a tension between the two verses, a dissonance that invited intrepid scholars to reconcile the apparent contradiction or celebrate the paradox. Yosef and his fellow Pharisees never shied away from these challenges. It was their great delight to look into the mind of HaShem. The Torah was always their first means of so doing.

Yosef found his ruminations interrupted when Yeshua and Yochanan entered the house from the workshop in a bustle.

"Shimmy is saddled up and ready to go, Abba," Yeshua said. "I have all of the gear and provisions that we might need for a couple of days."

"What are you talking about, son?" Yosef asked. Although, he knew the answer to the question even before he asked it. He could see the posture of readiness on both his son and his nephew, the conspiratorial expressions on the faces of his wife and in-laws. However, he couldn't simply go along with the assumption of an impromptu journey. Yosef needed to hear it.

"We all discussed it this morning, Yosef," Zechariya responded. "Yeshua plied us with his reasons for submitting to your direction last night. None of us like it, mind you. But we see the sense in it. After we discussed it for a time, it seemed good to us and to Adonai that the lads would both go with you, that they should be together."

Yosef stared at them in blank disbelief.

"You are all agreed," said Yosef as he made a demonstrable glance toward Miriam, "that I would take our two boys, introduce them to a Zealot, and solicit him for their martial training?"

"Like Uncle said, Yosef," Miriam replied, "we don't like it, but we can see your reasoning. And Yeshua was very convincing this morning."

Yosef was perplexed as he turned his gaze toward Yeshua.

"Well, how do you figure how far we would have to travel?" Yosef asked.

Yeshua and Yochanan exchanged a sideways nod and a shrug together as they looked to each other.

"You said that these training grounds are all over Yisrael, Abba," Yeshua responded. "And you haven't been away in a long time. We just figured that this man and his company couldn't be much more than a day's journey away. Otherwise, how would you have crossed paths with him, and how would you know where to find him?"

Yosef stared at his son in that regular sensation of bewilderment and familiarity.

"Besides," Yeshua offered, "we can always pack more or resupply along the way if we were wrong."

The father of the messiah looked around the room, waiting for someone to say something, as if this had all been a very impolite ruse. However, everyone looked back at him, waiting for him to respond. Yosef thought that the discussion had been going well the night before, but he had also gone to bed assuming that there were still several things to deliberate. Miriam had given space to his suggestion, but she hadn't fully conceded things yet. Then to find Zechariya and Elisheva suddenly wanting Yochanan to be a part of the expedition? And what did Yeshua say that was so compelling? It was too much to process all at once. Nevertheless, there they all were, ready for him to accept it and move on with the plan.

Eventually, the good carpenter gathered himself and nodded thankfully to everyone. He still wasn't sure how they had come to this point, but he was glad for it all the same. Gratitude would have to take the place of understanding.

"How about we set off after I've finished my breakfast?" Yosef suggested. Everyone agreed, Yeshua and Yochanan more heartily than the rest.

"Is there anything else that you'd like us to prepare before we leave, Abba?" Yeshua asked.

"No, son," Yosef said wryly, "it sounds like you have everything under control."

Everyone goodbyed for a long while. The mothers were profuse with hugs and kisses and well-wishing. Zechariya clasped his hands behind Yochanan's neck and prayed right upon the skin of his forehead, kissing him as he sought HaShem's blessing over their journey.

"May it be Your will, Adonai, our God, that You lead us toward peace, direct our steps toward peace and uphold us in peace. May You rescue us from the hand of every enemy and ambush along the way. May You send blessing in my handiwork, and give us favor, generosity and mercy in Your eyes and the eyes of all who see us. Blessed are You, Adonai, Who listens to prayer."

Eventually, they were finally permitted to set off up the winding path with Shimshon, saddled up for their haul. The three men each toted a modest satchel over their shoulders as well, and they all carried walking sticks. Yosef had also instructed the boys to tuck their work-knives into their belts beneath their cloaks.

The carpenter had done so himself. Every once in a while, he found himself checking to make sure the blade was still where he had fastened it in its sheath. The night before had been liberating in ways that he was continuing to count. It was also true that the day before taught him to walk a little more warily all the same.

At the outskirts of Natzeret on top of the town, Yosef whistled Shimshon to a halt and addressed the boys.

"Are you sure about this?" he asked. "There's no shame in reconsidering or setting off another time."

"Oh, come on, Uncle!" Yochanan ejected. "If we turn back now then they'll never let me go!"

Yosef and Yeshua laughed at the impetuousness. The father looked at his son as they chuckled, asking the same question with his face once again. Yeshua slapped his cousin on the back and nodded at his father. They were all set and ready to go, no more questions about it.

The group descended into the valley and traveled north through the farmlands of Natzeret's residents. The steppes of vineyards were to the east, cut into the rockface of the mount. The other crops were planted westward within the hollow of the valley. The final harvest before winter would soon be upon them.

The breeze was crisp and the air was clear. They traveled for hours without any need to take a break, ascending and descending the gentle slopes of the wilderness. On a few occasions, Shimmy would pause and munch at the tall grasses along the way. Whenever the donkey did so, the men didn't attempt to hurry the beast but instead had a snack for themselves as well. The going was pleasant in every way.

At one point, Yosef considered the sheer mental and physical toughness of Yeshua, behaving as he had the night before, rallying the family and rustling the donkey for the journey that morning. Had he not been there for the horror of it, Yosef would never have known that his son had been assaulted and subjected to a most troubling ordeal only the day prior. Did anything unnerve the child?

Yeshua and Yochanan were up the road several paces from Yosef, talking about the Kingdom and forming their schemes, as usual. Yosef walked alongside Shimshon with one hand on his mane, stroking the creature affectionately as he gathered his thoughts. The donkey had been a valiant companion.

As the carpenter allowed his thoughts to roam, he realized that the only instance in which he had seen Yeshua overtaken by his emotions was that heart-rending afternoon only a month or so prior. They had never revisited the issue, but Yosef wished that they had. How could the mention of such a dire vision go unrepeated?

Even on that day, when Yeshua insisted that he had foreseen the manner of his death, the calm that came over him after his outburst erased any trace of disquiet in the lad. No one could have known that anything had ever been wrong with him, not having been there to see his grief. Not even Miriam suspected anything that very night.

Yosef could not understand how it was that Yeshua kept such a perfect composure over his inner being. It was not the case that the child was unemotional, as their many recent interactions had proven. Yeshua felt many things, perhaps everything. At times it seemed as though he felt them more than anyone else. But how was it that he was never overtaken by those sensations? The boy was self-governed in a way that Yosef had never encountered in any other man that he had ever met, not even the likes of Zechariya, or, for that matter, Hillel himself. The conundrum strained credulity. Yet Yosef had lived with Yeshua every day since he had been born. There was nothing fake in him whatsoever. Children did not simply grow up without ever erring or forgetting themselves. Nevertheless, impossible as it was for the carpenter to comprehend, the proof was in the manner that Yeshua lived his entire life. Nothing false was in him. Only goodness shone through his being.

Far to the north of Natzeret and several hours away from home, Yosef saw an old fig tree on a hilltop away from the road. He knew they had come into the region of the Zealots, but he wasn't sure exactly where to head from here. The shade of a tree in the late afternoon sun was as appealing a spot as any to consider the next leg of their journey.

"How about we take a rest for a spell, boys," Yosef said as he led Shimshon up the hillside.

The boys turned from the road without question and followed Yosef uphill. They had made no complaints the entire way. Even so, they were glad for a respite, and they were always glad to scramble up a tree for a few figs whenever the opportunity arose.

Yosef stood at the base of the tree and caught tosses from the boys in his outstretched cloak. They were between the early and the late season, but they were able to discover a few figs that were ripe for the picking. It was just enough to settle in with.

They disburdened and unharnessed Shimshon before sitting

down to feed themselves. Grasses at the base of the tree were suffi-
cient for the donkey's appetite, so they tethered him on the other side.
Almost right away, Shimmy knelt and lied down beneath the shade.
He was glad for a rest too.

All three of the men leaned their backs against the tree and
enjoyed their fresh-picked figs. They still had water in their keeping to
abate their thirst, although they knew to be careful with the contents
as well. It was the perfect spot for leisure on any day, all the more so
in the middle of a journey.

"Blessed is He for the tree and the fruit of the tree," Yosef said, to
which the boys responded "Amen."

In quiet, they appreciated the sky in unison. With that shared
sense that travelers instinctively develop, they felt their togetherness
even more keenly for the many things they enjoyed with one another
without having to say so. Within that unspoken solidarity, they felt
like lords of creation.

Yosef found his eyelids heavy all of a sudden, realizing that the
sequence of days had left him rather spent. Being honest with himself, he had yet to recover from the day of the pergola build and the
party that night, not to mention the treacherous day and night that
followed. Finding himself tired several hours into a journey immediately thereafter, he became gentle with himself and surrendered to
the weariness. He still had not guessed where to head next, after all.

"In shalom I will both lie down and sleep.

For You alone, Adonai,

        make me dwell in safety."

The psalm was the last thought that he had as he drifted down and
away into his dreams.

The father of the messiah awoke to the disorientation of not knowing how much time had passed in his sleep. Yeshua and Yochanan

had dozed as well, having laid their heads on his shoulders after the carpenter was quite secure in his slumber, so much as to never have stirred until that moment. When Yosef regained the focus in his eyes, he saw a man's silhouette standing before them, against the red evening sun only a few handbreadths over the horizon.

"Greetings," Yosef said. "Have we found ourselves beneath the shade of your tree, sir?"

"Indeed, citizen," the man replied. "What is your business in these parts? Besides the current... hiatus?"

Yosef was becoming more alert, but he was still bleary-headed from the nap. He lifted his right hand to shield the sun from his eyes. The face was instantly recognizable as the man was unforgettable.

He looked like a young man who had somehow already lived the span of an old man's years. His face was hard, like a man of battle, also that of a man overly familiar with hunger. His eyebrows were thin and his nose was sharp; his cheekbones were high and stark. Even his features gave the impression that he would use his face as a weapon without flinching if it ever came to it. His frame was taut with muscle and sinew, like a sun-stained sailor returned from a long voyage. The man reminded Yosef of the Roman soldiers, only leaner and without their luxuries. His tallit was frayed with tzitzit that were all but worn away to the knots. And if it were possible, he seemed to wear his small tefillin with something like disdain.

"Ah!" Yosef exclaimed. "It seems you are my business, my friend! We met in Natzeret months ago. I spoke to you of my son. My name is Yosef, son of Ya'akov. Do you remember?"

The man did not reply but only looked over the two boys who were then rousing themselves from their naps. Yeshua and Yochanan each raised their heads off Yosef's shoulders and sat up straight. They straightened even more once they realized the presence of a stranger standing before them. Each of them looked to Yosef for reassurance.

"Which one is your son," the man asked at length, "and who is the other one."

Yosef stood up to make the introductions more formally. The boys stood as well. The man remained unmoved.

"This is Yehoshua, my son," Yosef said, "and this is my nephew Yochanan, son of Zechariya."

The three of them stood waiting as the man said nothing in return. He looked over the boys like a man does when he is considering the purchase of a pack animal. Yosef wondered at what qualities he could ascertain from such a cursory survey.

"I don't see the resemblance," the man challenged.

"Yes," Yosef conceded. "He takes after his mother's appearance." The good carpenter had offered that reply more times than he could remember, in response to assertions both more and less polite than the one before him. He winced a little inside every time it happened. But it had become a familiar query to manage, albeit hurtful. No one could know their secret. Yosef reminded himself of that single truth for so long that it had become an unyielding refrain that echoed within the chambers of all his considerations.

The man offered nothing in reply, neither acceptance nor refusal. He only continued to look at them. Yosef wondered who should be talking, or whether this unsettling audience was the only way that it could be. How many intruders or impostors had this fellow contended with before, Yosef wondered.

"So," the man bellowed at last, "the two of you have come of age and you think you're ready to slay some Romans, is that it?"

"All I know," Yochanan blurted in his characteristic recklessness, "is that the Romans must be cast out of our Land. If that means that we burn everything to drive them away and then build it all back up, fine. If it means we kill them by the legions before they tire of their losses, I don't care. If it means the whole of my life before we see them gone, then I am willing. Whatever the cost, I am ready to pay it."

"Oh!" the man said with enthusiasm, "there is a fire in you, boy. I like that. But we will have to teach you to tame it, lest it burn you alive and your fellows besides. Will you accept that discipline? To control the blaze that keeps your spirit hot?" It was the first display of hospitality that the man had offered since their encounter.

"You will find me ready for a great many things, sir," Yochanan replied, his voice was set like iron. He did not like his worth or his abilities being called into question.

"We can work with you," the man laughed. He seemed to be relaxing with them at last. "What about you, boy," gesturing to Yeshua. "Are you prepared to fight and die for your nation, for your people?"

Yeshua looked upon the man in silence. Yosef had seen this behavior, many times before. He would answer in his own time, not at the prompting of a peremptory adult.

"May I see your hand, commander?" Yeshua asked.

"What?" the man replied, indignant.

"I would like to see your hand," Yeshua repeated.

The man looked to Yosef for some explanation, but it had become Yosef's turn to remain imperturbable. The carpenter only looked upon Yeshua, at ease with his violation of custom, but unsure of what to expect. Yet, Yosef did know something of what to expect – and it would surely be something amazing.

Yeshua placed both of his hands out, upturned, as if waiting to receive alms. The man glanced at Yosef once more, still not receiving reassurance of any kind. Then he relented and placed his right hand within Yeshua's grasp.

The young messiah studied the man's palm. He forced the man's fingers closed and looked at the knuckles of his fist; he felt the man's forearm; he touched the man's elbow. The man was obviously uncomfortable, but never displayed any viciousness at the examination. Yosef could see that the man had begun to wonder whether Yeshua was addled in the head.

"You are a Benjamite," Yeshua said at last. "Your expert skill with the sling is apparent."

The man made the biggest face that he had worn yet. He was truly impressed. But he suspected trickery of some sort.

"All right, young man," he said, "you have determined my tribe. Impressive. What else do you suppose that you know about me?"

"What skill you lack with the sword you compensate for with ferocity," Yeshua rebuffed.

The man's face darkened. He had become more impressed, but also more embarrassed. A boy did not simply say such a thing to a warrior. He opened his mouth to speak, but Yeshua interrupted him.

"Your left hand is injured, is it not?" Yeshua asked, even though his conviction was clear in his question.

"By the Name, boy," the man gasped. "You are a shrewd one. I don't know how much soldier there is in you yet, but you'll make a fine scout at the very least."

As the man was talking, Yeshua stepped close, within the man's footing, and raised a hand to his chest. He paused, as if listening to something no one else could hear. Then his eyes welled up and tears rolled down his cheeks, although his voice remained clear and strong.

"The Romans murdered your wife," Yeshua soothed, "I am so sorry for your loss and your pain."

"What is this!" the man shouted at Yosef, backing away in a fury. "You bring me a boy that plays at being a prophet!"

"I play at many things, Benjamite," Yeshua interjected, "but prophecy is never one of them."

The man began to shout again, but Yeshua raised both hands high and lifted his voice above everyone.

"Peace, commander, be still!" Yeshua ordered. To Yosef's great surprise, the man stopped, perhaps only in shock that a thirteen-year-old had just behaved as he did. Yeshua spoke to him further before the man could rally himself.

"You do not want to be known anymore," Yeshua continued, "not since your life was stolen away from you. You mean never to love again so that you can never again know loss. I cannot heal that which you keep hidden, but I can learn from your training regardless. You would have me as a willing student.

Still, I think that you are unsatisfied, but not with us. So, I will answer the question that you have tucked away. This question you have not dared to ask of your most trusted accomplices. You have not even mustered the courage to ask it of yourself. How many men have you pressed about their willingness to fight and die on behalf of Yisrael? However, you never pose the question that you most want to know, so much that the words to your own yearning have eluded you.

Yet, I would tell you this: I am willing to die on your behalf for no other reason than because you are simply – you. Without the embellishment of a grand cause, that of a nation in peril, I would lay down my life for you only because you exist and because of the Father's great love for you. If you have no need of such devotion in your camp, then we will return to Natzeret and bother you no more.

Now you know the hearts of both myself and my cousin. How do you decide, commander?"

Yosef caught his breath. The boy was too much. Yet, somehow, despite the audacity of it all, it seemed like Yeshua was just enough.

The father of the messiah wondered if they would ever step away from the canopy of the fig tree. The man stood in perfect stillness and absolute silence. His very heart had been shown to him. Most men never wanted to see such a sight, much less be forced to reckon with it.

"We share the same name, young master," the man said at last. "I am Yehoshua, son of Abbas, born to the tribe of Benjamin, as you have said."

"Well," Yeshua smiled, "everyone calls me Yeshua... unless it happens to be Shabbat and my mother is around."

Then the elder Yehoshua laughed. It was a great laugh, a laughter born from bonfires in the wilderness and years' worth of dodging death's shadow. He laughed like a man who knew how to rally his troops.

"We have a few other Yehoshuas in camp, as well," the commander said. "We may have to come up with a nickname for you, unless you earn the right of primacy of your name."

"What shall we call you, sir?" Yochanan asked.

The elder Yehoshua reached toward Yeshua once more. Both of them clasped hands in earnest. Their respect was mutual. They had come to understand each other.

"They call me Barabbas."

Epilogue

THE NEXT DAY, Yosef was approaching the outskirts of Natzeret on his return trip home. Barabbas had prevailed upon him to leave the boys for a time, to which Yosef only agreed on the condition that they would be finished with their introductory examinations by Rosh HaShanah. After seeing Yeshua stand his ground with men that were trained killers, the father of the messiah was learning to worry about his son less. Of course, he was still returning home without the boys, which likely meant an argument and an earful. He was still learning to worry less about himself, too.

He stroked Shimshon's mane as if the donkey might be coaxed to kick such invisible concerns away from the path in from of them. He chuckled at himself, rueful. Maybe he'd find another fig tree to sleep beneath first.

However, homecoming thoughts would have to wait, as would the sleepy ones. About a mile outside of town, Yosef could see a Roman cadre standing in the road. Eight soldiers were there in all, plus a centurion's violent scarlet plume among them.

It was Gaius.

Perhaps they had come to arrest Yosef. It made sense, he had to suppose. At least they were not waiting for him at his home this time. But what of his home? He realized that Yeshua was safe, but what of the rest of the family? Too much could happen in two days' time.

"Halt, Jew!" one of the soldiers cried.

Yosef halted Shimshon. Both man and beast froze in their tracks. They waited.

Before any of the soldiers could approach them, Gaius called out in a commander's authority.

"My helm is heavy, Jew," Gaius bellowed in Greek. "I would have you carry it for me."

None of the soldiers moved, neither did Gaius. Yosef could only assume the onus was on him to approach. If he moved judiciously, perhaps he could assuage any potential hostility.

As Yosef walked toward the cadre slowly, Gaius issued a few terse commands in Latin. Immediately, the soldiers dispersed in units of four. One group jogged past Yosef and the other foursome trotted toward town. Each group took up their positions about a stone's throw away from their commander.

Only Yosef and Gaius stood together then, with Shimshon standing alongside the carpenter. The centurion placed his helm into Yosef's hands and began to walk. His pace was that of a commander's promenade, unhurried and lordly. The soldiers at both extremes instantly matched his tempo in lockstep. Yosef followed next to Gaius, unsure of what would come next.

Several minutes passed during the quiet march. Yosef's mind was racing with the possibilities. It seemed as though they had come to an understanding only a couple of nights prior. But this was the Roman Empire. The carpenter could only guess what might have transpired since then. Gaius may have received orders; the wounded legionnaire might have been prominently connected.

Then, as Yosef considered the parameters of the centurion's life, it occurred to him that the two of them were walking together in broad daylight, surrounded by Roman soldiers as it were. Perhaps the helmet was merely a ploy for those that looked on. It was a brazen thought, but something in Yosef's spirit rang true. Besides, he hazarded that at least one presumptuous utterance would be sufferable enough if he were out of line after all.

"Would you like to talk about Torah?" Yosef asked Gaius in Hebrew.

"I would like that very much," the centurion responded. He grinned at the ground, looking forward, hoping that Yosef would notice. Of course, the good carpenter saw it and grinned at the ground in return. They dared not smile at each other before the eyes of the soldiers' accompaniment.

"Where would you like to begin?" Yosef queried.

"Oh, by the Name!" Gaius exclaimed. "I have so many questions! Why did God find favor with Avram? Why is He so invested in the Land of Yisrael? Where did Melchitzedek come from? What happened to Moshe's body? When is the Prophet like him supposed to come?"

"My friend," Yosef smiled, "those are all excellent questions. But we have a problem."

"I'm terribly sorry, Yosef," Gaius stammered. "Is it improper to discuss Torah while handling a Roman's armor?"

"Nothing of the sort," Yosef reassured. "Nothing of the sort, my friend. No, the problem is that we are only a mile outside of town... and those are all two-mile-questions!"

Gaius looked at Yosef in disbelief and delight all at once.

"You might prevail upon me to carry your armor an extra mile or so," Yosef winked, "but can your legs handle the duration while your feeble Roman's mind races to keep up with the lessons?"

Gaius darted a glance at Yosef as he slapped down heavy on top of the helmet in his arms, nearly knocking it out of the carpenter's grasp.

"Heavy is the helm, Jew!" Gaius smirked.

"Weighty is the Torah, dog!" Yosef rejoined.

They both stifled their sniggers as though they were schoolboys trying not to be caught by the pedagogue. Each of them would be hard-pressed to restrain their impulses to goad each other even as they yearned to peer into the beautiful wisdom of Torah. The two men walked together in their newfound secret friendship, invisible in broad daylight, camouflaged by the enmity of their peoples.

Afterword & Acknowledgements

TO THE READER: Thank you, wherever and whoever you are. You could have spent your time on so many other tasks, with any number of other books and projects. The hours that you have given me in this space is a great gift. Truly, I am so grateful that you permitted my little creation here to inhabit any part of your life. If you like what you've read and would like to stay engaged, please visit my site at www.soulwrights.org. Perhaps it's possible that we would become friends.

The students of history and theology may find themselves with different interpretations than I have presented here. I have done my best to collate the Gospel accounts with the contemporaneous literature of that time. Dr. Kinzer has referred to some of my filling-in-the-blanks as retrojections from the Talmud and other such materials. That's a helpful way to refer to it. Wherever the interim remained gray, no matter how much I researched, I took the necessary liberty of imagination. If the reader has a better mosaic than I have assembled, then I welcome their convivial engagement.

One such potential divergence could be Yosef's livelihood. Recent archaeology as well as linguistic scholarship has shown that Yosef may very well have been a stone mason rather than a carpenter, or perhaps some amalgam of both skill sets and others besides. While these possibilities are intriguing, I did not find it conducive to the story to bring these elements into play within the narrative. For my part, I felt as though I was taking enough creative risks already. To let Yosef remain a carpenter, as he has been classically portrayed and understood, seemed like the best route. What's more, when the story first came to me, unsolicited, Yosef and Yeshua were engaged in nothing but fine carpentry. My task was to do my very best to work out the rest of the story from that moment of reverie and epiphany.

Other considerations would be the nature and relationships between the multifarious sects of 1st century Judaism. Ever since Israel has been revived as a nation-state, the landscape of Biblical scholarship has undergone significant renovations with every successive decade. The work is ongoing and shows no signs of relenting any time soon. Archaeology continues to yield manuscripts for translation as well as proofs and discoveries of the cities and townships and even persons. Much of my story has been informed by these intrepid scholars willing to do the hard work of revising classical understandings in the light of new evidence. As John Flavel said, "Antiquity is no passport for errors."

Should the reader find themselves wanting to learn more, I must recommend the voluminous and wondrous materials available from all of the teachers at First Fruits of Zion. The BEMA Podcast with Marty Solomon is another wonderful resource. Of course, the scholarly works of Dr. Mark Kinzer cannot be endorsed highly enough. I have learned more than I can recount here from each of these noble, brilliant, pious teachers. Should their thoughts have been misrepresented throughout the story in any way, then I am solely to blame. This is especially the case with Dr. Kinzer, who took the time to vet my story from a historical, scholarly perspective, and then provide instructive feedback.

Too many people require recognition in my life, and I hope that no one feels slighted if they do not find their names collected here in print. Tomes could be written about the wealth of personal influences that I have had in companionship. The following is the best that I can determine as to direct creative influences in the contents or inspiration of the book itself.